I Am America

JOURNEY TO A PROMISED LAND

A Story of the Exodusters

Book design by Jake Slavik
Illustrations by Eric Freeberg

Photographs ©: Library of Congress, 154 (top), 154 (bottom); North Star Editions, 155

Published in the United States by Jolly Fish Press, an imprint of North Star Editions, Inc.

First Edition
First Printing, 2018

This is a work of fiction. Names, characters, places, and incidents are either the product of the author's imagination or are used fictitiously, and any resemblance to actual persons living or dead, business establishments, events, or locales is entirely coincidental.

Library of Congress Cataloging-in-Publication Data
Names: Lassieur, Allison, author. | Freeberg, Eric, illustrator.
Title: Journey to a promised land : a story of the Exodusters / by Allison
   Lassieur ; illustrated by Eric Freeberg.
Description: Mendota Heights, MN : Jolly Fish Press, [2019] | Series: I am
   America | Summary: "Hattie Jacobs and her family join the Great Exodus of
   1879 in search of a better life in Kansas" —Provided by publisher.
Identifiers: LCCN 2018038112 (print) | LCCN 2018041143 (ebook) | ISBN
   9781631632778 (e-book) | ISBN 9781631632761 (pbk.) | ISBN 9781631632754
   (hardcover)
Subjects: LCSH: African American pioneers—Kansas—History—19th
   century—Fiction. | Freedmen—Kansas—History—19th century—Fiction. |
   CYAC: Family life—Kansas—Fiction. | Freedmen—Fiction. | African
   Americans—Fiction. | Frontier and pioneer life—Kansas—Fiction. |
   Kansas—History—19th century—Fiction.
Classification: LCC PZ7.1.L377 (ebook) | LCC PZ7.1.L377 Jo 2019 (print) | DDC
   [Fic]—dc23
LC record available at https://lccn.loc.gov/2018038112

Jolly Fish Press
North Star Editions, Inc.
2297 Waters Drive
Mendota Heights, MN 55120
www.jollyfishpress.com

Printed in the United States of America

I Am America

JOURNEY TO A PROMISED LAND

A Story of the Exodusters

By Allison Lassieur

Illustrated by Eric Freeberg

Consultant: Sharlene Sinegal-DeCuir, PhD,
Associate Professor of History, Xavier University of Louisiana

JOLLY
FiSH
PRESS

Mendota Heights, Minnesota

Chapter One

April 5, 1879

Dear Diary,

We had a spelling bee at school today. Me and Josephine were tied for first at the end. Then Miss Banneker gave us the hardest word. Chrysanthemum. I did right terrible with it. I lost my head after the "R." Jo got it right though. I'd have been mad if she weren't my best friend. But it's important that I get my spelling right if I am to become a teacher. Oh my! I can't believe I just wrote that down. It's a good thing Bram can't read yet because I haven't told that secret to anyone. But it is my deepest desire . . .

Hattie

$\mathcal{I}$t was one of those late-spring days when the world is bright and warm, and everything feels possible. Hattie ran the ten crowded blocks from the First Baptist AME Church toward home, her heart pounding hard from excitement or the running, she wasn't sure which. She expertly dodged the dirty pools of water in the street, weaved past the butcher's store that always smelled of blood, and ducked into a narrow alley. It was crisscrossed with a web of clotheslines that dipped heavily with the laundry her mother took in for extra money.

Hattie stopped short, breathing heavily. "Mama!" she called. "I'm home!"

"In the back, baby," came her mother's voice.

Mama was bent over an enormous black iron cauldron, pushing a wooden paddle back and forth in the bubbling, gray water. The familiar scents of wood smoke, lye soap, and steamy clothes hung in the air. She saw Hattie and paused in her work, smiling.

Hattie threw her arms around her mother in a quick hug, feeling those thin, strong arms wrapped around her like a comforting blanket.

"Mama, guess what? Miss Banneker picked me for the recital! I'm going to read a poem in front of everybody!"

Mama beamed with pride. Her rough hand, cracked and hardened through years of work, stroked Hattie's cheek. "Oh, baby, I'm so proud of you," she said.

"Will you come?" Hattie asked, still out of breath from the run. She knew what the answer would be, but she asked anyway, just to hear it.

"I wouldn't miss it for the world," her mother replied. "Papa too. And Abraham, if we can keep him from squirming through the whole thing."

Hattie grinned. She knew how much stock her parents put on learning. When they were enslaved, they hadn't been allowed to learn to read or write. After the Civil War, one of the first things they'd both done was go to school.

"Speaking of your papa, he needs his lunch, and you do too. It's on the table."

Another hug and Hattie dashed through the narrow doorway at the end of the alley. She took the rickety stairs two at a time up to their small two-room apartment. The front room served as kitchen and dining room. The black iron cook stove took up most of the space, along with a table and chairs. The back room held the big, soft bed for

Mama and Papa. Hidden beneath it was the trundle bed for Hattie and Abraham.

Every day when school let out at noon, Hattie came home to take Papa his lunch. Mama always had the food carefully wrapped and waiting. Hattie grabbed the packet and sniffed. Biscuits and sausage, Hattie's favorite.

"Bye, Mama!" she called. But Mama was bent over the tub again, wearily wiping sweat and steam from her forehead.

Papa's blacksmith shop, a tiny building not much bigger than a shed, was down the street and around the corner. The words JACOBS AND SON BLACKSMITH were painted black above the wide double doorway. Abraham was only three, but Papa had high hopes.

Hattie was usually greeted with the ring of hammer against iron, but today, the shop was quiet. A horse she didn't recognize stood quietly in front, his expensive saddle gleaming in the midday sun. Maybe a new customer, Hattie thought. Nashville was a big town, with lots of horses to shoe and wagons to fix. Everybody, black or white, knew Papa was a good blacksmith and an honest man.

A white man Hattie had never seen before stood talking to Papa in the doorway. He was older, with long, greasy gray hair peeking out from a shapeless hat. Papa leaned against the door jamb, his huge arms crossed against his chest.

"General Anderson over at Magnolia Run is anxious to have you work for him again," the white man was saying. "He sorely needs good blacksmiths. He told me personally how much he misses you."

"Is that so, Rees?" Papa spoke slowly. "I was his slave from the time I was ten years old until emancipation came to Tennessee in 1864. That was fifteen years ago. I'm not about to go back to that place."

Rees's watery blue eyes narrowed. Hattie held her breath, clutching the packet to her stomach.

Rees pulled a grubby envelope out of his pocket. "He still wants to hire you, against my better judgment." He smirked as Papa opened the envelope and began to scan the pages.

"This is a big order," he said finally. Rees's eyes widened in surprise. Hattie realized with a start that he hadn't expected Papa to know how to read.

"I require half payment up front," Papa said, his tone polite. "I think five dollars is fair."

Without a word, Papa calmly straightened up to his full height of six foot two, his blacksmith arms like small tree trunks against his sides. Rees sputtered and mumbled curses but handed Papa a handful of crumpled bills and coins.

"You're short fifty cents, Rees." Papa said.

"You'll get the rest when you're done!" he shouted.

Papa gazed at him. Then he picked up the huge iron hammer resting against the side of the shop. His forearms bulged as he casually swung it up and rested it on one shoulder.

Rees glared at Papa with such hatred that it seemed to pour out of him. After a moment, he turned on his heel and took off. Hattie sighed with relief as she slid her hand into Papa's large, rough one. Papa smiled down and gave her hand a comforting squeeze.

"Gotta keep an eye on that Rees," he said, watching Rees ride away. "He's the General's head assistant, and he's rotten to the core." Shaking his head, he wiped his hands on a rag from his back pocket. They found a patch of sun in front of the shop for their picnic. Between bites, she told her father the good news.

"I'm right proud of you!" Papa exclaimed, wiping biscuit crumbs from his mouth. He glanced up as a shadow fell across them.

"More company," he said under his breath.

Hattie looked up too, worried that Rees had come back. But the elderly black man who stood in front of them was nothing like the watery-eyed Rees. He was well dressed in a crisp suit, with long, iron-gray hair that curled in waves to his shoulders.

He smiled and held out his hand to Papa.

"Nat Jacobs? I'm Benjamin Singleton. Folks call me Pap. I've been anxious to speak to you."

Papa set down his biscuit and, with a puzzled expression on his face, stood up to shake Singleton's hand. "Do you need a blacksmith?"

Singleton chuckled. "I don't, but I know of many who do." He pulled a paper out of his pocket and handed it to Papa.

"What is this?" Papa asked.

HO FOR KANSAS!

Brethren, Friends, & Fellow Citizens:
I feel thankful to inform you that the

REAL ESTATE
—— and ——
HOMESTEAD ASSOCIATION
Will Leave Here the
15th of April, 1878,

In pursuit of Homes in the Southwestern Lands of America, at Transportation Rates, cheaper than ever was known before.

For full information inquire of Benj. Singleton, better known as old Pap, NO. 5 NORTH FRONT STREET.

Beware of Speculators and Adventurers, as it is a dangerous thing to fall in their hands.

Nashville, Tenn., March 18, 1878

"It's a flier I made up last spring," Singleton replied. "You know things are bad for the black man here in the South. It wasn't so bad during Reconstruction, when Union troops kept order. Now that they've gone, things are getting worse. There's been more lynchings than ever. Men who speak out, disappear. White landowners force black farmers to rent their land at inflated prices. Then they cheat them, refusing to pay fairly for their crops. Our people can't get ahead, no matter how hard they try."

"But I'm not a farmer," Papa said, with a note of sadness.

"You could be," Singleton replied, waving the paper. "In Kansas, black people are free to better themselves. The government is giving away farmland to anyone— ANYONE—willing to put their backs into making a go of it. I've been personally leading groups to Kansas. I took several last year. I'm looking for families to join me this year."

"And how do you propose we get all the way to Kansas?" Papa asked.

"Steamboat," was Singleton's instant reply. "Steamboats up the Mississippi will take you straight to St. Louis. From there, you can get out to the settlements."

"I'd have to get myself and my family all the way to Memphis then. That's more than two hundred miles from here," Papa didn't sound convinced. "I've lived in Tennessee all my life. My daughter goes to school. My shop is doing well."

"But you can have a blacksmith shop in Kansas," Singleton continued. "There are good schools in Kansas. And whole towns where every citizen is like us. Every one!"

Papa shook his head. "Thank you for seeking me out," he said. "But I'm not interested in uprooting my family for a wild dream."

Singleton nodded. "I understand." The two men shook hands, and Singleton tipped his hat to Hattie, who was now standing next to her papa. "Good day, miss," he said.

Singleton went a few paces and then turned. "There's a meeting on Friday evening. We'll talk about Kansas and other things you may find interesting. I hope you'll consider attending." Then Singleton, whistling, turned back around and strode down the street.

"You wouldn't really move us all the way to Kansas, would you?" Hattie asked anxiously as they watched Singleton go.

"I expect not," Papa said. "Now, finish up your dinner and get along to Miss Bradford's house. Isn't she expecting you today?"

"I don't want to go!" The idea of being cooped up in that dark, old house mending tea towels on such a fine afternoon made Hattie want to scream. "Cain't I stay here and help you? I won't be a bother."

Papa folded Hattie into his huge arms. "There's nothing I'd like better," he began. "But Miss Bradford is a kind woman, and she pays you a fair wage for your work. God knows, we can use every penny."

Hattie knew better than to argue. She finished the last of her biscuit and set off.

At the end of the street, Hattie looked back. Her father was standing in the doorway of his tiny shop, arms crossed, watching her go. There was a look in his eyes that Hattie had never seen before. Pride, and sadness, but something more than that.

Fear.

Chapter Two

There wasn't much sunlight left to shine through the stiff lace curtains when Hattie picked up the last tea towel from the basket. A stack of freshly mended towels, napkins, and other small items sat in a neatly folded pile beside her chair. Hattie rubbed her eyes, and then squinted to thread the needle one more time. If she worked fast, she'd be done before the light was gone.

A rustle of silk and the scent of rose water came into the room and paused behind her, but Hattie didn't look up from her work.

"About done?" Miss Bradford's voice was low and scratchy, like she'd swallowed a handful of sticks that never went down.

"Yes, ma'am," Hattie replied, the steel needle sliding in and out of the fabric, trailing white thread behind. "Just have this one left."

The old woman picked up one of the mended pieces. She squinted at it through her spectacles, which were perched on the end of her nose like a tiny wire bird. "I could make stitches this fine once myself." She sighed and dropped the towel into the basket. "Back before the war, when life was so different."

Hattie kept silent and sewed faster. Miss Bradford loved talking about her girlhood. But Hattie always got a funny feeling in her stomach as the woman described her plantation home, with its rolling fields of cotton and dozens of slaves working from dawn until dark.

"There!" Hattie tightened the last stitch and broke the thread with her even, white teeth. "Good as new, Miss Bradford." She stood up, feeling her backbone crackle. The only thing she wanted was to go home. But there was one more thing to do, something her mama insisted on.

"Is there anything else you need, Miss Bradford?"

"As a matter of fact, yes." Miss Bradford always had something extra for Hattie to do.

Hattie tried not to sigh out loud as she followed Miss Bradford into the kitchen. After she drew two buckets of water from the well, wiped down the table, and washed a tub full of dishes, Miss Bradford seemed satisfied. The old woman's twisted hands painfully unknotted a threadbare handkerchief, and several coins dropped into Hattie's palm.

"Thank you, ma'am," Hattie said. She knew without looking that the pay didn't include all the extra housework. But all she could do was grit her teeth and remember her father's words. *We can use every penny.*

It was almost completely dark by the time Hattie was on the street, flying home as fast as her legs could carry her. It was at least a mile, through parts of town she'd rather not go through in daylight, let alone at night.

Tonight, though, the city was quiet. She rounded the last corner and sped through the back alley and up the stairs. Wonderful smells of fresh-baked biscuits and fried meat filled the apartment as she closed the door behind her.

"Hattie!" Papa was already at the table, feeding Abraham a piece of biscuit. "We was getting mighty worried. Miss Bradford keep you late again?"

Hattie nodded as she slid into her chair. A plate of fried pork and brown beans appeared before her. "She made me do the dishes this time. I expect they'd been sitting there for days."

Mama sat down with her own plate with a sigh of relief. "Now, Hattie, she's an old woman and her rheumatism is bad. She cain't do such chores, and that no-good housekeeper don't show up half the time."

"I don't know why I have to do all the work," Hattie said bitterly, between bites. "She never pays me for the extra."

"Because the good Lord gave you a strong body and a quick mind," Mama said. "And you'll use those gifts to help others in need."

She didn't understand how a white woman who lived in a big house could be someone in "need," but Hattie kept eating and said no more about Miss Bradford.

Papa nodded as Abraham tore across the room, dropping biscuit crumbs like snow on the clean, worn wood floor. Hattie watched Mama quietly eating her supper as Papa grabbed Abraham in a tickly hug just to hear him giggle. Her heart was suddenly so full of love, it felt like it would burst.

After the table was cleared and the dinner dishes done, Mama lit the lamp and pulled her knitting out of the basket by the stove and Papa pulled out the trundle bed in the back room. Hattie crawled beneath the colorful quilts as Papa slid Abraham in beside her. His tiny, warm body curled up against Hattie's back, and he was snoring in an instant.

Mama and Papa talked softly in the front room, their voices rising and falling in a duet with the gentle *click click* of Mama's knitting needles. Hattie listened until her mind wandered comfortably to her favorite daydream. It was the one no one else knew about. In the daydream, she was a teacher just like Miss Banneker, standing in front of a classroom. Hattie wanted to be a teacher with all her heart. But teacher's college cost money, more than her family could ever hope to make.

I'll just have to work hard, Hattie thought drowsily as her thoughts began to float away. She was almost asleep when

Papa uttered a word that cut through the fog in her mind. *Rees*. Her eyes flew open and she held her breath, listening.

Papa told Mama about Rees and the order from the General.

"I didn't want to say yes, but Lord knows we need the money."

"There's something else," Papa continued. He told Mama about Singleton and Kansas and the meeting.

"Nat!" Mama exclaimed. "It's our dream come true! You've always wanted a bit of land for your own, to farm."

"That's true," Papa said. "But Kansas? That's a long way from here."

There was silence for a time, and Hattie's eyes grew heavy. Then Mama laughed, a sweet sound that roused Hattie into wakefulness once again.

"I have a bit of news of my own," she said. "Another one of our dreams is going to come true. In about six months."

Papa gasped. "Are you sure?"

Mama laughed again. "Women know these things," she said, happiness in her voice. "Just think of the chance this child will have in Kansas!"

The kerosene lamplight disappeared, plunging the apartment into darkness. Mama and Papa stepped quietly into the bedroom, careful not to bump the trundle bed. After a few minutes, the big bed creaked and moved as her parents settled in. Hattie imagined Mama nestled in Papa's arm, close and warm.

"I'll consider the meeting, for you." Papa said. "But can you believe a whole town with nothing but black folks? I can hardly imagine it."

"I can." Mama's voice was sleepy and far away. "I dream it every day."

Chapter Three

$\mathcal{M}$iss Bradford must have run out of tea towels to mend because she didn't send for Hattie the rest of that week or the next. Instead, Hattie spent every afternoon after school at the shop. Papa's hammer rang all the way down the narrow Nashville street as he worked to fill Rees's order. One by one, Papa fashioned hinges, latches, locks, and keys. He made strong, straight nails. There were also cooking pots and pothooks and fireplace tools. Hattie wasn't allowed near the red-hot coals while Papa was working, but she didn't mind. Blacksmithing was a loud and dirty business. She was perfectly happy to sit outside, practicing her recitation. Teachers needed to know how to do such things.

When the sun began to set, Papa would appear, covered head to toe in ash and sweat. She always had a brown jug full of water waiting. He'd drink deep, hang up his battered leather apron, and scrub the grime from his skin. Then together, they'd walk home.

Friday afternoon was particularly sunny and warm, and Hattie was tired of practicing. Papa was restless too. After lunch, he stood up and wiped his head with a cloth.

"What do you say we quit early?" Papa winked. "It's too fine a day to waste."

Together, they set off down the street. They dodged delivery wagons and carriages *clop-clopping* in the streets. The smells of fresh-baked bread and horse manure filled the air. Two busy blocks later, Papa opened a shop door, its small brass bell tinkling merrily as they entered.

The pharmacy was long and narrow, with tall shelves on both sides. Rows of jars brimmed with colorful liquids and syrups. Others held dried plants and flowers. Wooden crates were stacked here and there. Bags of loose tobacco sat near boxes of cigars, their spicy scent tickling Hattie's nose. Bottles stood at attention along the shelves, with words like *camphor, lavender, belladonna,* and *Balsam of Peru* written in fancy letters on their labels.

"Hallo, Nat," A short, white man with a bald head trotted from a doorway behind the counter. "What can I do for you today?"

"Here's the pots you ordered," Papa placed a parcel on the counter. "Hattie, this here is Mr. Banks."

"Nice to make your acquaintance," he said, smiling. "How about you go over there and pick out a piece of candy?"

Stunned, Hattie looked at her father. "It's all right," he said, smiling. "I need to talk to Mr. Banks about some business."

Hattie slowly walked to the end of the counter. The large glass jar was filled with hard candies in every color of the rainbow. She was debating between a red and an orange candy when she heard Papa say the name "Rees." Hattie's ears perked up to listen. But before she could figure out what Papa was saying, the brass bell tinkled again. A white woman walked in, followed by a boy a year or two older than Hattie. They pushed past her to the counter where Papa and Mr. Banks were talking.

"I'm here for my order," she said. The men stopped talking.

"I'll be with you in a moment, ma'am," Mr. Banks said.

"I want my order now," the woman demanded in a loud voice, glaring at Papa. He looked at her calmly, and then nodded to Mr. Banks.

"I'm happy to wait a bit," he said. "You go on ahead and help this lady out."

"I will NOT," Mr. Banks replied, turning to the woman. "Mr. Jacobs was here first, and I have business to conduct with him. You are welcome to wait your turn. We should be finished directly."

"Mister? You call that man 'mister'?" she sputtered, overcome with anger. "Come, Thomas, we're leaving," she spat, turning on her heel. As they passed Hattie, the boy gave her a kick.

"Oww!" Hattie cried, dropping the candy as the two left. She could hear the sound of the boy's laughter before the door slammed shut.

Papa was at her side in an instant. She buried her face in his shoulder, tears of pain and embarrassment making a dark stain on his rough shirt.

"Why did he do that?" Hattie asked, sniffling. "I didn't do anything to him."

"Some people have meanness clean through," Papa said. He put a finger under Hattie's chin and raised her eyes to meet his. "You are proud and strong, and you must ignore folks like that."

"Here," Mr. Banks pulled a huge lollipop from a jar on the top shelf. "I hope you accept my apologies, miss. That'll never happen again in my store." He looked at Papa. "You have my word."

"Thank you, John," Papa said.

Mr. Banks waved Papa's thanks away. "Don't mention it," he said. "And as for the other thing, yes, I'll take care of it for you."

Papa nodded.

"What do you say we head home and show Mama your lollipop treasure?" he said, smiling at Hattie.

April 20, 1879

Dear Diary,

Today wasn't such a good day. A horrid boy kicked me when Papa and I were in Mr. Banks's store. Mr. Banks was very kind though. Even though he is a white man. I think he and Papa are friends. He even gave me a lollipop! But Mama made me give some to Abraham. I broke off a big piece and gave it to him but he spit it right out! Three-year-old brothers are a trial to the soul.

I hope the new baby has better manners.

After supper Papa told us he had decided to go to Mr. Singleton's meeting. I don't want to go to Kansas. I love school and I love Miss Banneker. But Mama says she wants to leave Nashville.

I'm afraid for Papa tonight. I've heard stories of what happens to black people who go to meetings like this. One man went missing after such a meeting. They found his body a week later, strung up in a tree. The thought that that might happen to Papa makes my blood run like ice. Mama says he'll be fine. He's strong and well-liked by black and white folks alike. I'm not so sure. I think I'll wait up for him, if Mama lets me.

Hattie

Chapter Four

The candle on the table had burned to a tiny nub when Hattie woke with a start. She had fallen asleep at the windowsill, waiting for Papa to return. Mama was wide awake, sitting in her rocker; Abraham a heavy, snoring lump on her lap.

"What time is it?" Hattie asked.

"Past midnight," Mama replied in a low voice, her brow furrowed with worry. "I should have put you to bed hours ago, but . . ."

They heard footsteps on the stairs.

"Papa's home!" Hattie exclaimed, running to the door just as Papa came in.

Hattie leapt into his arms, hugging his neck like she'd never let go. He crushed her to his chest in a bear hug. She didn't mind.

"What's that smell?" Hattie asked suddenly, wrinkling her nose.

"I expect it's Mr. Mabry's hog pen." Papa put Hattie down and kissed Mama on the forehead. He gathered Abraham up and walked to set his sleepy form on the trundle bed. Then he came back and sat at the table with a sigh.

"Where were you?" Hattie couldn't contain herself any longer. "What happened? Are we going to Kansas? Why do you smell like a hog pen?"

"Let your papa be." Mama handed him a cup of warmed-over coffee.

"Mary, you should have seen it," Papa said, taking the cup gratefully. "There must have been a hundred black men at that meeting. It did my heart good to speak with so many respectable folks."

Papa told them how black residents and businessmen from all over Nashville had gathered to talk about the exodus to Kansas. "Mr. Singleton has gone back and forth to Kansas for a few years now," Papa explained. "He takes groups of folks with him, his 'exploring committees,' he calls them."

He drained the coffee cup and sat back. "Singleton thinks nothing will get better for black folks in the South. At least not in our lifetimes."

"Is that what you think too, Papa?" Hattie asked worriedly.

"There was a time when I couldn't imagine being free. And now we're free."

"Well, the way I see it," Mama spoke up, "It may have only taken the Yankees four years to set us free, but it took more than two hundred years of our people living in slavery to get to it."

"Your mama has a point," Papa said with a weary smile. "And it's time for you to be in bed."

Instead, Hattie climbed into his lap and snuggled against his wide, warm chest. "You never told us why you smell like a hog pen."

"Oh, that!" Papa's arms curled around her. "Well, a bunch of us had a bit of excitement after the meeting broke up," he said. "We was chased most of the way home, and I hid in the hog pen for a time."

Hattie gasped as Mama exclaimed "Nat!"

"Now don't go gettin' all upset," Papa said. "No one got him and I'm fine."

"What happened?" Hattie's stomach did a little flip.

Papa shrugged, "Some white folks don't like it that black folks were meetin' and talkin' about leaving Tennessee," he said, his voice light. Hattie wasn't fooled, though, and neither was Mama.

Hattie laid her head on Papa's shoulder. "I'm just glad you're home."

"Now you get on to bed," Papa said. "We've both got a busy weekend. Rees is coming for his order tomorrow, and you've got your recital Sunday."

Hattie slid between the covers of the trundle bed, gently shoving Abraham's legs away from her side. She closed her eyes and tried to ignore the ache in her stomach. She wasn't sure if it was from nerves or something else. *It's the recital,* she decided. But in her dreams, she was hiding in a pig pen, terrified in the dark.

Chapter Five

The next day was gray and chilly, and it matched Hattie's mood. She sat grumpily on the stump outside Papa's shop, eyes closed, straining to remember the words of the poem she'd chosen.

> Thank God for little children,
> Flowers on the earth . . .

"No, that ain't right!"

> Thank God for little children,
> Pretty flowers by the way . . . way . . .

"That ain't right either!"

She peeked at the folded paper in her hand.

"*Bright flowers by earth's wayside,*" she grumbled. "I'll never be able to get this in my head by Sunday. Why didn't I pick an easier poem?"

Her head ached and her back was stiff from sitting so long. She jumped off the stump and went into the shop. Papa was busy packing up some things for delivery.

"Papa, why do you work so hard for such a dreadful man like Rees?"

"It's about doing your best," he said. "What would happen if I made shoddy hinges, or weak horseshoes?"

"They'd break."

"Doors would fall off. Horses would go lame. Word would get around that my work weren't no good. Rees wouldn't get blamed, I would. And rightly so."

"Always do your best, Hattie," he said, tucking another bundle into the box. "If you can respect your own self and know you did your best, no one else matters."

From outside came the sound of a wagon rattling to a stop. Before she had a chance to take a step, Rees stood in the doorway. He fixed his watery eyes on Papa.

"I'm here for the order," he growled. He was wearing a threadbare Confederate jacket, dotted with dark grease spots. A huge revolver hung in a holster on his hip.

"Here it is," Papa replied, glancing at the weapon. "All packed and ready to go." He handed Rees a paper with columns of items written in a steady hand. "This here's a list, and the boxes they're in. You see that everything the General asked for is here."

Rees snatched the paper from Papa's hand and squinted at it for a moment. Then he shoved it into his pocket and gave a whistle. Two grimy white men appeared and began loading the boxes onto the wagon.

Papa straightened up to his full height. "I've marked down the cost of each item on that paper. I'll be taking the rest of the payment now."

Rees broke out into a grin, his yellow, uneven teeth showing. "And I'll be taking this order for what I done paid you," he said. "You think you're as good as us, don't you? Well, you ain't."

Just then, they heard shouting from outside. Rees's eyebrows shot up. His hand went to his gun as he ran toward the sound.

"Stay put." Papa pointed to Hattie, and then rushed out. Hattie couldn't stand not knowing what was going on. She crept to the doorway and peeked out.

Rees and his two assistants stood in the middle of the dirt street, surrounded by men. Hattie recognized Mr. Banks from the store and other shop owners from the neighborhood. Some were black, others were white. All of them were armed with rifles or guns. Hattie held her breath.

"What's this?" Rees was red-faced with fury.

"Well, it's like this," Mr. Banks began. "Us merchants here on this street, we watch out for one another. Thieves aren't tolerated. Mr. Jacobs here was a mite suspicious that such a thing might happen to him. He told us to watch out for thieves. Do you know about anyone tryin' to make off with merchandise that isn't his?"

"No!" Rees's voice squeaked with fear as he gripped his gun. "This is all mine, fair and square. Already paid for. Stand aside."

"'Fraid not," Papa said. Hattie was shocked to see him holding his ancient rifle. It was already old when he picked it up from a dead rebel during the Battle of Gettysburg. "This man, Rees, only paid me half. He owes me five dollars." He looked Rees straight in the eye. "And fifty cents."

"Well, then, Mr. Rees, it's time to pay up," Mr. Banks smiled, but it wasn't friendly. "Or you can return these boxes to Mr. Jacobs and call it a day. What do you say?"

Rees's face was red as a beet, and his scraggly hair seemed to be standing on end. If the tension weren't so thick in the air, Hattie would have laughed.

"You think you got me beat, don't you?" he said in a voice so low, Hattie could barely hear him.

He began to slide the gun from its holster. The air instantly filled with soft clicks as the men cocked their weapons, ready to fire. Rees paused, eyes wide.

No one moved.

Then slowly, Rees took his hand off the gun. He reached into his coat and pulled out a thin leather wallet. He counted out five dollars and fifty cents and slapped it down on Hattie's stump.

"This ain't over, Nat," Rees hissed as he climbed into the wagon. The two other white men jumped into the back with the crates, glaring at the crowd. As they pulled away, Rees stood up, shouting so loud, the words echoed down the street.

"THIS AIN'T OVER!"

The street was silent except for the rattle of the wagon until it disappeared around the corner. The men gave a great collective sigh, breaking the tension.

Hattie ran to her father, who was shaking hands with Mr. Banks.

"I'm beholden to you, I truly am," Papa was saying.

"Nat, you don't have to thank us," Mr. Banks said. "I was speakin' the truth. We don't allow thievery in our neighborhood."

"You'd do the same for us, Nat," another man said.

"If you ever have another dust up with that maggot, you send for us," another said. Slowly the crowd broke up and went back to their own stores and shops, leaving Hattie and Papa alone.

"You knew Rees wasn't going to pay, didn't you?" Hattie asked.

Papa shook his head. "Not exactly," he replied. "But I was sure he was gonna try something. That's why I asked Mr. Banks to keep an eye out when Rees showed up. He must have told the others." He gazed down the street where Rees and the wagon had gone.

"Hattie, do something for your papa," he began. "Don't go out alone for the time being. I'll walk you to and from school. If you go to Miss Bradford's, one of us will fetch you." Hattie nodded as a chill went up her spine. Rees was right, and they both knew it. This wasn't over yet.

April 22, 1879

Dear Diary,

How does a heart go bad, I wonder? It ain't always from terrible things that happen to a person. Papa and Mama were born and grew up in slavery. They don't talk much about those days but I know they were horrible times. Papa was sold away from his family when he was just a little boy. He never saw his parents again. I can't think how I would feel never to see Mama or Papa again.

But Papa's heart is so good. There ain't a mean bone in his body, or Mama's neither. Then there are folks like Rees. His heart is filled with hate. Others too. I see how they look at us when we walk down the street sometimes. Like it's an insult to them that we exist. But folks like Mr. Banks and the other shopkeepers are kind. Being nice and caring for folks doesn't always come easy though. Maybe it's easier to hate?

Hattie

Chapter Six

"Get a move on, Hattie," Mama called from the front room. "We don't want to be late! Abraham, hold still!"

From the howls coming out of Abraham's mouth, Mama must be scrubbing his face, Hattie thought with a weak smile. Her stomach churned as she sat on the bed and buttoned up her shoes, freshly polished with lamp black. The poem raced through her head, over and over.

Thank God for little children
Bright flowers by earth's wayside . . .

"Oh, Hattie dear, you look a picture!" Mama exclaimed as Abraham squirmed off her lap. She had on her Sunday best too, a deep-red calico dress with delicate silver buttons. Her hair was held in place with her most prized possession: a carved tortoiseshell comb studded with tiny, black jet beads. Hattie knew it was a special occasion when Mama wore that comb.

The door flew open as Papa came in. He stopped dead, staring. Then he grinned.

"My, my, I'm the luckiest man to have such beautiful women! I might faint dead away with pride!"

"Oh, Papa, you look splendid!" His suit wasn't new, but Mama had carefully washed and brushed it the night before.

"Why thank you," he replied. He hefted the well-packed lunch basket that was sitting on the kitchen table. "Shall we?"

They set off to the church, a sweet honeysuckle breeze filling the air. Hattie loved walking through the city on Sunday. The crowds were gone and the streets were quiet. When the small clapboard church came into view, Hattie's stomach did a heave. Knots of people in their Sunday best stood, chatting, near carefully tended flowerbeds of daffodils and tulips. A familiar face broke away from the crowd.

"Jacobs! So good to see you again!"

"Singleton," Papa said, warmly shaking his hand. "I'm surprised to see you here today."

"I've been speakin' about Kansas at churches around Nashville," he replied.

"Hattie!" Josephine waved madly from the church steps. "Over here!"

Gratefully, Hattie raced to the church and gave Josephine a hug.

"I could hardly keep my oatmeal down this morning," Josephine said in a rush, her bright-green hair ribbons shining in the sun. "All these people!"

"Don't even say it," Hattie nodded and pressed her hands to her stomach. Just then, the church bell rang to call everyone inside. Hattie and Josephine grabbed hands and made their way to the front pew, where the students sat.

The recital would happen after the church service, and then there was a picnic. Hattie's mind whirled through the hymns, then the prayers, and then Reverend Jackson's sermon. Almost before she knew it, the reverend said the final prayer, and then closed his worn Bible.

"Now I know ya'll didn't come here just to hear me preach," he began, to soft laugher. "This is a special day. Not only will we hear from some of the brightest students in our school, but we also have a guest, Mr. Benjamin Singleton."

Singleton told them about Kansas and the opportunities to be found there. "I've helped to establish three towns in Kansas, and all are doing well," he said. "Kansas has land—plenty of land! I urge you all to consider leaving

Tennessee. There is nothing here for black folks but pain and unfairness."

Finally he sat down, and Hattie's teacher, Miss Banneker, rose. She was tall and elegant, with delicate hands. She was the first black Yankee Hattie had ever met, and the only grown-up she knew who had never been a slave.

"I am very proud of these children," she said in her soft voice. "They've worked hard for you today."

One by one, the students got up in front of the congregation. The little ones sang songs or showed pictures they had drawn. A group of boys put on a wild play about pirates and treasure. Then it was Hattie's turn.

"Miss Hattie Jacobs is one of the best students in school," Miss Banneker said as Hattie stood beside her, trembling. "She has prepared a poem."

Miss Banneker gave Hattie's hand a squeeze and sat down. Hattie looked out over the crowd of faces, and her mind went blank. Then she caught sight of Papa, standing in the back. He smiled and nodded, his eyes shining with love. Hattie took a deep breath.

"This poem was written by Miss Frances Ellen Watkins Harper," she began. "She was born free in the North. Before the war, Miss Harper was a teacher. She helped slaves escape on the Underground Railroad. This poem is called 'Thank God for Little Children.'

She glanced at Miss Banneker, whose lovely smile felt like sunshine on Hattie's heart. Hattie smiled back, and suddenly the words were there.

> Thank God for little children,
> Bright flowers by earth's wayside,
> The dancing, joyous lifeboats
>
> Upon life's stormy tide.
> Thank God for little children;
> When our skies are cold and gray,
>
> They come as sunshine to our hearts,
> And charm our cares away.
> I almost think the angels,
>
> Who tend life's garden fair,
> Drop down the sweet wild blossoms
> That bloom around us here.

Thunderous applause shook the little church. Hattie sat down, cool relief washing over her. Josephine was next, and everyone clapped for her too. Then the program was over and the reverend threw open the doors to the beautiful afternoon. The men quickly set up makeshift tables out of boards as the women laid out platters of ham, chicken, fried catfish, biscuits and gravy, greens, and more cakes and pies than Hattie had ever seen. She and Josephine filled their plates and found a shady spot in the tiny graveyard beside the church.

"I'm glad that's over!" Josephine said, her mouth full of sweet potato.

Hattie nodded. Miss Banneker caught Hattie's eye and smiled, then came over to them.

"Hattie, may I talk to you?"

Hattie, brushing the biscuit crumbs from her dress, stood up and followed her.

"Have you ever thought of becoming a teacher?" Miss Banneker asked. "You would make a fine teacher."

"Yes, ma'am, I have," Hattie said slowly. Being a teacher had been a dream for so long, it felt strange to hear her voice say it out loud. "But teacher's college is mighty expensive," Hattie continued, trying to keep the sadness out of her voice.

Miss Banneker smiled kindly. "Yes, it is expensive," she agreed. "Have you ever heard of something called a 'scholarship'?"

When Hattie shook her head, Miss Banneker continued. "A scholarship is an award that colleges give to exceptionally good students. It pays for their college education."

Colleges give money away? The idea had never entered Hattie's mind. "Do you think I'm good enough?" she asked.

"You're more than good enough. If you worked hard, you could qualify for a scholarship."

Hattie's breath caught in her throat. "Oh, Miss Banneker!"

Suddenly there was a commotion as a rider tore down the street toward the church. "Nat Jacobs! Is Nat Jacobs the blacksmith here?" he yelled, his hat flying off his head.

"I'm Nat Jacobs!" Papa called to the rider.

"Come quick! Your shop is on fire!"

Chapter Seven

It was as if a cannon had exploded into the crowd. Several women cried out as Papa and a dozen men took off toward the shop. The reverend quickly hitched a wagon, and his wife took Abraham from Mama's arms, urging her to go. Soon, Hattie and Mama were racing through Nashville, Mama praying and crying the whole way. Hattie smelled the smoke as they got close. The sight that greeted them when they rounded the corner made her heart stop.

People were running and shouting everywhere as black smoke billowed down the street. Firemen aimed a water hose at the flames, but only a tiny stream of water spit into the shop. A bucket brigade line snaked around the block, people passing buckets of water down the line to the fire wagon. Next to the tower of fire, their efforts looked small and useless.

"Papa!" Hattie screamed, jumping from the wagon. "Papa!" The terror she'd felt when he went to the meeting gripped her heart again. This time, would she lose him for good?

Not if I can help it, she thought fiercely as she ran down the street.

"Hattie!" Mama's voice cried from behind her, but she ignored it. Hattie knew Papa would try to save his tools. They were his most prized possessions.

Hattie ran down the street and around the corner. He probably went through the alley into the back, she thought wildly, where the flames weren't so bad.

Strong hands grabbed her from behind, holding tight. Hattie screamed and jerked free, stumbling onto the rough dirt street.

"You can't go in there!"

It was Mr. Banks. Grime and soot covered his face and clothes.

"Where's Papa?!" Hattie cried, scrambling to her feet, her eyes stinging and watering from the smoke.

"I couldn't stop him," Mr. Banks said, his voice choking.

Hattie took a step toward the shop, and a loud *whoosh* filled the air. A wave of heat blew past her as flames engulfed the wall. The building seemed to tremble. Then a loud crash shook the alley as the shop collapsed, sending smoke and sparks into the sky.

"PAPA!"

A figure emerged from the smoke, dragging a charred wooden crate. He stumbled, and then fell to his knees, coughing violently.

Hattie and Mr. Banks were beside him in an instant. His nice suit was burnt and torn. Angry red burns covered his arms.

"Nat, you crazy fool, why did you go and do that?" Mr. Banks grabbed Papa under his arms and heaved him to his feet. "You coulda been killed in there!"

Papa, still coughing, leaned on the shorter man. "Had . . . *cough* . . . to get . . . *cough* . . . tools."

By now, Singleton and several others had appeared in the alley. He ducked under Papa's other arm, and he and Mr. Banks together half-carried, half-dragged Papa away, Hattie right behind them.

"Oh, dear Lord!" Mama cried as she saw them emerge from the alley.

"I'm fine, Mary," Papa coughed again.

Hattie ran into Mama's arms and burst into tears. Mama hugged her tightly and then pushed her at arm's length. "Don't you ever do such a fool thing again, do you hear me, Hypatia Florence Jacobs?" she cried, her tears making streaks on her cheeks. "I near died of fright when I seen you run around that corner."

"I'm sorry, Mama," Hattie repeated over and over, her head buried in Mama's shoulder. She was still shaking with fear, and her legs felt like jelly.

"It's all right, baby," Mama said, stroking her hair. "You're all right, your daddy's all right, that's all that matters."

"Where's Abraham?" Papa asked, looking around anxiously.

"He's with the reverend's wife," Mama replied, standing up. "He's safe, thank the Lord."

By now, there was nothing to do but watch, helplessly. It seemed like they stood there for hours watching the flames gradually die, leaving a ruin of burnt timbers.

Hattie stared at the wreckage and wondered for the first time how it had started.

"Was it the forge, Papa?" Hattie had always feared Papa's forge, which glowed red and hot as he worked.

"Jacobs," Mr. Banks appeared, carrying something. "I found this in the back."

It was a noose, singed and burned.

"Rees!" Papa gasped.

Mr. Banks shook his head, sorrow in his eyes. "You'll never be able to prove it. And even if you did, what would anyone do about it?"

The unfairness of it all hit Hattie like a punch in the stomach. Papa looked at the burnt rope for a long time. Then he stretched his arm back and threw the horrible thing into the dying flames.

"I think it's time to talk to Singleton about Kansas."

BLACKSMITH SHOP BLAZE CALLS FIRE DEPARTMENT

The fire company was called to the shop of Nathanial Jacobs, a colored man, yesterday around three o'clock. The shop was destroyed but no one was hurt. The cause of the blaze was sparks from the forge. It was not insured.

April 25, 1879

Dear Diary,

Papa's shop is gone. Burnt to the ground. There's nothing left for us here in Nashville. Papa says he doesn't have the money to rebuild the shop. He doesn't want to work for someone else either. He says he had his fill of that when he was enslaved. Mama wants to go to Kansas now more than ever.

   I'm so numb I can barely hold the pen or write these words. I'll put out the candle and try to sleep but I feel like crying instead.

                                                        Hattie

Chapter Eight

May 2, 1879

Dear Diary,

I haven't written in a while on account of being so busy. The last two weeks have flown by, packing and planning the trip to Kansas. We've already sold most of our things. Papa used the money to buy a wagon and a mule named Old Jeb. Old Jeb is smelly and ornery and I don't like him much. But he'll pull our wagon to Memphis where we'll get on a steamboat to Kansas. I'm trying to get excited about riding a steamboat but I can't. I feel cold and numb. I want to cry all the time. But mostly I'm angry.

I'm angry that the shop burned down. I'm angry at Mama. Why does she have to be so happy about going to Kansas? But I'm angry at Papa most of all. If only he'd not antagonized that horrible Rees, maybe the shop would still be standing. Every time I look at Papa, the anger bubbles up into my throat like acid. I want to scream, or stomp my feet, or run away to live with Josephine's family. I want to be in school but instead I'm packing. If I don't study hard I'll never be good enough for a scholarship. I'm not even sure if there is a school where we are going. My dreams are gone, and it's all Papa's fault.

Mournfully,
Hattie

On Hattie's last day of school, Miss Banneker had a going-away party. She even made a cake, but it tasted like dust to

Hattie. Afterward, her classmates somberly presented her with an autograph book they'd all signed.

"Oh, Hattie!" Josephine cried, bursting into tears. "I may never see you again!"

Hattie hugged her as hard as she could, her breath catching in her chest.

"Maybe you will," she managed to say finally. "Didn't your daddy say he liked what Mr. Singleton was saying? Maybe you'll all come to Kansas too."

Josephine sniffed and wiped her nose with the hem of her dress. "I don't think so," she said. "Ma refuses to talk about it. Here."

She thrust a small box into Hattie's hand. "It's paper and envelopes. You write me every day, you hear? I want to know everything that happens. Promise?"

"I promise," Hattie replied, her own tears threatening to spill over.

Papa was waiting by the door when the last bell rang. He smiled, but Hattie couldn't move. Today, when she walked out that door, she was never coming back.

"I cain't!" she cried. She ran to Miss Banneker and buried her face in her dress. "I'll never go to school again. I won't ever be a teacher now!"

"Oh, my dear Hattie," her teacher said, folding her into a hug. "Of course you will. There are schools in Kansas, good schools I'm sure."

"I have something for you too," she continued, handing her a hard, square package. Hattie ripped the paper to reveal a slim, leather-bound book.

"*Poems on Miscellaneous Subjects* by Frances Ellen Harper Watkins," she read slowly. "This is the book my poem came from, isn't it?" She looked at her teacher in wonder. "I've never owned my very own book before," she said, running her fingers over the shiny, gold letters. "Thank you, Miss Banneker. I'll keep it forever!"

"Remember, my dear, you can do anything if you want it badly enough," she said, her smile so sweet and sad, Hattie thought her heart would break. "I will miss you."

"Let's go," Papa's voice broke through Hattie's misery. Hattie gave her teacher a final hug and ran out the door.

They walked slowly through the busy Nashville streets. When they reached Miss Bradford's stately home, Papa stopped.

"Go on in and say goodbye," Papa said. "I came by on my way to fetch you. She wants to see you. She's waiting for you in the front parlor."

Hattie swallowed hard and nodded.

"Miss Bradford?" Hattie called, pushing open the heavy oak front door. "It's me, Hattie."

"In here, dear," came that scratchy voice. She was sitting by the window, her skirts billowing around her like a lake of silk.

"You're leaving, then," Miss Bradford said, not taking her eyes off the window. Hattie had never noticed how thin and pale her lips were. They stretched across her face, surrounded by a thousand tiny wrinkles.

Hattie nodded. "Yes ma'am."

Something about the forlorn look in Miss Bradford's eyes broke through Hattie's own misery. She put her hand on Miss Bradford's shoulder. She was so frail. The old woman stiffened, then sighed. She pressed some paper into Hattie's hand.

"I'll miss . . . your fine stitching," she said, her eyes bright with wetness. "Go in peace, child."

May 9, 1879

I went to say goodbye to Miss Bradford today. She slipped something into my hand when I left, but I didn't look at it until I got home. She gave me five dollars! It makes me a little ashamed of all the times I complained about the extra work.

I'm not sure why, but I didn't tell Mama or Papa about the money. Instead, I sewed it into the hem of my dress. Now it's hidden and no one but me knows it's there. I'm going to save it for college.

Hattie

The next morning dawned cool and clear. After a meager breakfast of cold beans, the Jacobs family gathered the last of their things and finished loading the wagon. Then it was time to go. Hattie gave Abraham a boost into the wagon as Papa helped Mama in. Hattie climbed onto the seat beside Papa so Mama could keep an eye on Abraham in the back.

"He-ya," he said, snapping the reins. The wagon jerked as Old Jeb the mule set off through the crowded morning streets. No one paid them any mind.

Like any other day, Hattie thought bitterly. *How can the world go on when my world is over?*

They drove past the shop, now nothing more than a pile of blackened timbers. A fresh wave of anger made Hattie's hands tremble, but she clenched her fists and kept it inside. Papa looked straight ahead, his head held high. Neither of them looked back.

Slowly the city fell away behind them, replaced by woods and green fields. The sun rose higher, and the cool morning air grew warm. Papa had agreed to meet Singleton a few miles outside town. They were joining the group he was leading to Kansas. It was late morning when they spotted a cluster of wagons and people by the side of the road.

"Ho, Jacobs!" Singleton called. The group had gathered under the shade of a huge oak tree. Everyone was oddly quiet. Hattie sensed tension. When Singleton spoke, she understood why.

"I've got bad news," Singleton said. "I won't be able to go with you. But you'll be just fine."

Papa looked stunned. "Memphis is more than two hundred miles from here! And that's just to the steamboats. What are we to do when we reach Kansas?"

"I'm truly sorry, Nat," Singleton replied, and he did look sorry. "There's no help for it. I must stay here for another few days, and you all don't need to wait. But I'll meet you in St. Louis in three weeks. You have my word." Singleton gave the group the best route to follow, along with some precautions, then turned his horse and disappeared back toward Nashville.

Everyone stared at each other, unsure. Then Papa said "We're Nat and Mary Jacobs. This here is Hattie, and the hellion in the back is Abraham." Abraham picked that moment to let out a howl, and laughter rippled through the group.

There were introductions all around. Four other families had made the decision to go to Kansas. The Coopers included a mother, father, and two teenage boys. The Bakers had no children. The Williams family had one girl about Abraham's age.

"Welcome, fellow Exoduster." A young man in a floppy hat waved to Papa. "I'm John Ferguson, and the missus here is Beulah." A pretty young woman with a baby on her shoulder waved shyly.

"What's an Exoduster?" Hattie asked curiously.

John laughed. "It's the name the papers done give us folks who are leaving for Kansas," he said. "Like the great Exodus in the Bible, when Moses led the slaves to freedom."

"Seems fitting," Mama said. "I guess that makes Kansas a Promised Land!"

"Let's just hope we're not lost in the wilderness for forty years," Papa said wryly. Mama laughed, and Hattie started. It was the first time Hattie had heard that sweet sound since before the fire. In all the rush and anger, she'd almost forgotten what Mama's laugh sounded like. Something inside Hattie loosened, just a little. Maybe things might be all right after all.

Amid the neighing of horses and the rattle of wagons, the Exodusters turned west, toward the Mississippi.

May 10, 1879

Dear Diary,

We left Nashville for good today. I thought I would cry but the tears didn't want to come. Maybe I'm all cried out. A few miles outside town we met up with other families going to Kansas. They seem nice enough. There aren't any children my age though. One family has two teenage boys. Another family has a girl about the same age as Abraham. In a way I'm glad. I'm not very good company right now.

Hattie

Chapter Nine

For the next three days, the Exodusters made good time. Hope and excitement were in the air, and Hattie couldn't help but catch a little of it. The beautiful late-spring weather helped too. The days were warm and bright, the deep-blue sky filled with puffy, white clouds.

Late on the third afternoon, the group stopped to rest. Papa and the other men huddled together, talking in low voices. When Papa came back to the wagon, he had a worried expression.

"There's been talk of a mob of white men roamin' the woods, looking for trouble," Papa said. "Ferguson says they're mad at all the Exodusters for getting out of Tennessee. Seems they're takin' issue with all their labor leaving."

"What are we going to do?" Mama asked.

"Not much we can do," Papa shrugged his shoulders. "But we decided not to stop until after we cross the river. It's too risky to make camp on this side."

Everyone was quiet as they set out. The colorful sunset faded, revealing a riot of stars in a dark, moonless sky. They never traveled at night, and the strangeness of it mixed uncomfortably with the anxious lump in Hattie's stomach. A single torch at the front of the line was the only light. Hattie stared at the feeble red-gold flame bobbing in front of them, a tiny shield against the darkness.

She heard the river before she saw it: a low, deep hiss that was almost lost beneath the *chirrup* of crickets. A collective sigh of relief moved through the group. They'd heard the river too.

As they got closer, something in the air changed and the crickets fell silent. The hairs on Hattie's arm rose.

"Papa?"

"Shhhh."

Abraham whimpered. In the back of the wagon, Mama hushed him.

A yell echoed through the trees, then another. Suddenly a wall of torches and men blocked the road in front of the bridge. Hattie clutched Papa's sleeve and gasped.

The men had no faces. Their heads were covered with kerchiefs, their hats shoved low. Their rifles pointed straight at the group.

"That's far enough." One of the faceless men stepped forward, his gun cocked.

"We ain't done you no harm," Mr. Cooper, the older man with the teenage sons, responded. "We're just passin' through."

"Not tonight you ain't," the man said. "You folks go on back to wherever you came from, and no harm will come to you."

"Hattie," Papa leaned down to whisper. "Take Abraham and Mama. There's a shallow spot about half a mile upstream with an old barn on the other side. Go there and wait for me."

Trembling, Hattie grabbed her diary and tucked it into her waistband. Then she slid down and helped Mama and Abraham out of the wagon. Abraham squirmed madly,

trying to get out of Hattie's arms. She set him down hard and clamped her hand over his mouth.

"Now you be quiet, you hear?" she hissed. Abraham was so startled that he stared at her, wide eyed. Mama gave him a fierce look as they snuck quietly back down the road to a grove of trees. They made their way through fields and woods, circling around until they reached the riverbank. Finally Mama let out a little gasp of relief.

"We're in the right place," she said. "There."

The old barn rose before them like a shadowy ghost. It had collapsed on one side, and half its roof was open to the sky. Now all they had to do was get to it.

Mama beckoned to Abraham, but Hattie stopped her. "I'll carry him, Mama."

Before she lifted him onto her back, she stooped low and looked him in the eyes. "Hold onto this tight now, you hear?" Then she tucked her diary into his waistband.

Abraham's wide eyes stared back and her and he nodded. Hattie bent low, and Abraham climbed onto her back, his small arms clinging to her neck.

"Hold tight, Bram," Hattie said, straightening her legs.

Mama gripped Hattie's shoulder so hard it hurt, but she was too scared to care. Together, they waded into the swiftly rushing water.

Hattie gasped as her feet hit the icy-cold water and stumbled. Her mother's steady hand tightened its grip on her. The water came up to her knees, then her waist. Hattie struggled against the current, hoping her feet wouldn't go out from under her.

"You're doing fine, baby," Mama said, pulling her forward. "Almost there."

A few more steps and they scrambled up the bank, soaking wet and covered with dirt. Mama took Abraham by one hand and Hattie by the other and led them inside the barn. They found a stall in the back, the splintery floor scattered with piles of old hay and dead leaves.

"You're soaked clean through," Mama murmured. They pushed the leaves and hay into a pile, and Hattie collapsed in a heap, her teeth chattering from the cold. Abraham curled up and fell asleep. Mama gathered Hattie in her arms.

"We'll be safe enough here tonight," she said. "He'll be here soon."

Hattie tried to ignore her wet stockings squishing in her shoes and looked up through the broken roof. There were so many stars that the black sky seemed to glow with them. Somehow, the hugeness of the universe gave her comfort. She relaxed against Mama and sent a prayer for Papa to the heavens.

Chapter Ten

May 14, 1879

Dear Diary,

Last night was one of the longest I've ever known. We ran into some trouble. A group of men blocked the road and wouldn't let us cross the Mississippi River. Me, Mama, and Abraham escaped to an old barn. My stockings were wet and Abraham snored all night. But being hungry was the worst feeling of all.

When I woke up this morning, Mama told me she'd sprained her ankle crossing the river. I was scared. But she was so calm she helped to make me calm too. She told me *to find something useful in the barn and I came across an old bucket. It didn't have a handle and there was a hole in the side. But Mama plugged the hole with a bit of her petticoat and I got some water from the river. The river looked a lot bigger than it had in the dark! The water tasted cold and fresh. We drank and washed our faces. Now there's nothing to do but wait for Papa to fetch us.*

Hattie

*H*attie watched the shadows move across the dusty barn floor as the hours passed. Her worry grew into a sick lump in her stomach that hurt more than being hungry did. It was late afternoon when she heard a sound outside. Before she could move, a familiar face peeked inside. With a holler, Papa raced into the barn.

"Thank the dear Lord you're safe," he exclaimed, crushing them in his huge, strong arms.

"What happened, Papa?" Hattie gasped. "Where are those men?"

"Gone," he replied. "But it was a close one, I won't deny it."

Papa told them the Exodusters turned back, but the mob followed them to the county line. Before they left, the faceless men ransacked the wagons and took all the food.

"What about your tools?" Mama asked worriedly.

"They didn't notice the box under the seat in the dark," he said, a note of relief in his voice.

"Once they were gone, we came right back to the bridge and crossed over," Papa said, helping Mama up. "So I high-tailed it here as soon as I could."

She winced as she tried to put weight on her foot. With one motion, Papa swept her into his arms.

"The rest of the group is waitin' for us a couple miles down the road," he said to her. They slowly picked their way through the fields, resting from time to time. An hour later, they reached the road. The Coopers and the Fergusons were the only ones there.

"Where is everyone?" Hattie asked. The Williams and the Bakers were gone.

"Some folks decided to go on back for good," Mr. Cooper said. "Cain't say I blame them."

"There should be a store between here and Memphis where we can get supplies," Papa explained as they climbed into the wagon.

"How much farther is it to the Mississippi, Papa?"

"A week, if we don't run into any more trouble. But there's good news. The steamboats are free! The government is payin' for our passage to Kansas."

"Are you sure?" Mama asked, always skeptical. "Mr. Singleton didn't say nothin' about free passage."

"Well, no," Papa admitted. "But Cooper is sure of it. Ferguson says he saw it in the newspaper."

"It's true, Mrs. Jacobs," Ferguson said happily. "Not only that, but the government has set aside the whole state of Kansas for us black folks. They'll give five hundred dollars to anyone willing to go there and work the land."

That afternoon, it began to rain, and continued until the next afternoon. Papa fashioned a top for the wagon from their tent, but it didn't keep out much of the wet. Hattie, Abraham, and Mama huddled miserably under it, trying not to think about food.

"There's a town comin' up in a mile or two," Papa said. "I'm sure they'll have a store."

The rain stopped, and the men went off to find the store. A little while later, they returned, empty-handed and silent. Without a word, the group moved on. At the next town, they tried again to buy food and supplies. Again, they came back to the wagons with nothing.

"Word's got around that we're passin' through," Papa reported when he returned. "No one will sell to us."

Every town they stopped at, no one would sell them supplies. The next afternoon, Papa managed to hunt a few scrawny squirrels. Mama and Mrs. Cooper made a watery stew to share, but it barely satisfied people's hunger.

Later, Hattie climbed into the wagon to sleep, ignoring her empty stomach. She tried to remember the last time she'd felt full. Then it came to her in a rush of memory:

her family sitting around the table at their house, warm biscuits and salt pork on their plates. She choked back a sob, not sure if she was crying for her lost life or the food she had taken for granted. Then a tiny, dark idea came into her mind.

The quarter moon was high in the clear night sky. Hattie waited for the others to fall asleep. Then she quietly crept from the wagon, careful not to wake anyone. As soon as the camp was out of earshot, she broke into a run. The cool night air felt good against her face. Soon her destination came into view: a small farmhouse they'd passed earlier in the day. A barn sat behind it.

She paused, unsure and afraid. She was about to turn around when her stomach rumbled, loud and painful. Abraham's sad face swam before her, pinched with hunger.

I'll only take a little, she whispered. *Please forgive me.*

Slowly she crept into the barn. It was warm and dark, and smelled of hay and manure. Cows shuffled and moved in the stalls. She found a few empty bags and some boxes, but nothing to eat. As she was about to leave, she heard a low *cluck cluck*. It came from some boxes along the far wall.

Hattie's heart leapt. She slid her hand gently into one box, and her fingers found a hard, oval object. An egg!

Quickly, she searched every box and was rewarded with seven large eggs. Carefully, she wrapped them in her skirt.

"Now if I can only get them back without breaking," she said out loud to herself, heading for the door.

"You're not going nowhere, thief."

A figure stood in the doorway, a pitchfork pointed at Hattie's head.

Chapter Eleven

*H*attie froze. It felt like someone had poured a bucket of water on her head.

"P-P-Please don't kill me," she stuttered.

"Who in tarnation is that?" The voice was surprised, but still angry. "Come out and show yourself."

It took everything Hattie had to take that step, then another. Rough hands grabbed the scruff of her neck and dragged her outside.

"Why, you's nothing but a child! What are you doing in my barn?"

It was too dark to see much about the woman other than she was tall. And she was white. She gripped that pitchfork like she was itching to use it.

"I—I—I—" Hattie's arms trembled so badly that the eggs rolled out onto the ground with a splat.

"NO!" She dropped to her knees. She frantically
searched the ground, but all she found were gooey raw egg
and broken shells, mixed with dirt.

"Who are you, child?" The voice was a great deal less
angry now. "Are you one of them Exodusters they've been
talkin' about?"

Miserably, Hattie nodded. It was quiet in the barnyard. At that moment, her stomach let out a loud rumble.

"I see," the woman said softly. An owl hooted somewhere in the distance. Finally, the woman leaned the pitchfork against the barn.

"Come with me," she said.

Slowly, Hattie stood up, her legs wobbly from fear. Without another word, the woman led Hattie to the back of the house and into a small kitchen.

"Sit."

Hattie obeyed, sinking onto a hard wooden chair. The woman lit the kerosene lamp on the table, and then busied herself at the huge black cast-iron stove. In the sputtering light, Hattie got a better look at her. She was older than Mama, she thought. This woman had wrinkles around her eyes and thin blond hair pulled back in a bun. Her night dress had definitely seen better days. But it was clean and neat, as was the kitchen.

In no time, the woman sat a plate of hot scrambled eggs, cold cornbread, and a thick sausage in front of Hattie. She devoured every crumb as the woman watched.

"What's your name, child? I'm Mavis. Mavis Robinson."

Hattie didn't want to tell this Mavis Robinson anything. What if one of those faceless men lived here? But the hot rush of fear and guilt had drained away, leaving her tired and worn out. The words came tumbling out. Hattie told her about the fire, Kansas, the horror at the bridge, and how no one would sell them food or supplies.

When it was over, Mavis sat back in her chair. "That's quite a tale," she said.

"Mam, who's that?"

A little girl appeared in the doorway in her nightshirt. She climbed into Mavis's lap, her big brown eyes staring at Hattie. Hattie stared back. Her skin was as dark as Hattie's. Her black, wiry hair stood up in clumps, just like hers did when Mama didn't braid it before bed.

Mavis put her arms around the girl. "This here's Hattie," she said, pointing to their visitor. "She came by for a bite to eat. Now you go on back to bed, you hear?" The little girl nodded and disappeared.

"That's my youngest, Annabel," Mavis said with small smile. "Her daddy, well . . ." she paused. "He had a run-in with those men. I ain't seen him since."

Mavis stood up abruptly. "Enough of that. Now, come with me."

Hattie followed her to a tiny pantry. Soon she packed a basket with a small bag of cornmeal, a tin of crackers, several plump sweet potatoes, a slab of bacon, and a packet of raisins.

"It ain't much, but it'll get you to Brownsville, at least," Mavis said, tucking in a half loaf of bread. "When you get there, tell your daddy to find a Mr. Henry Walker. He owns a store on the north side of town. He'll sell you whatever you need."

It all was too much bear. Hattie leaned against the pantry door and sobbed.

"I'm sorry I stole from you," she gulped, hiding her face with her hands. "I'm so sorry."

"Thievin' is a bad thing," Mavis said, handing Hattie a worn but clean handkerchief. "But it ain't no sin to do what you have to do to care for the ones you love."

Hattie nodded and wiped her face until the tears were gone.

It was still dark when they walked outside.

"Can you get back all right?" Mavis asked, handing Hattie the basket.

Hattie gripped the handle and nodded.

"Thank you," she whispered.

Mavis gave a curt nod. "I'd be obliged if you didn't mention where you got them victuals. I can't have hordes of hungry Exodusters at my doorstep."

"I won't," Hattie promised.

"Good luck, child." Then she was gone, the screen door slamming softly behind her.

To Hattie's relief, the camp was still asleep when she got back. Papa was sitting beside the wagon, waiting. He jumped up when he saw her.

"Hypatia Florence Jacobs, where on earth have you been? And where did you get that basket?"

Hattie rushed into her father's arms, joy and relief washing over her like a flood. After the whole story came out, Papa peered into the basket.

"You met an angel tonight, I think," Papa said in a low voice.

May 16, 1879

Dear Diary,

Mavis Robinson's food lasted until we got to Brownsville, just like she said. Papa and Mr. Cooper found the store and we got plenty of food to get us to the steamboats. The rain finally stopped too. There wasn't a cloud in the sky and it wasn't too hot. Our spirits rose with each mile closer we got to the mighty Mississippi.

There was much discussion between the adults about how to catch the steamboats. Some wanted to go into Memphis. Singleton had said there's a steamboat landing a few miles north of the city. Mr. Ferguson thought that we shouldn't bother going into *town when we can get right on the boat. Everyone finally agreed to his idea.*

We are all excited, even Abraham. He was screaming and running around like a wild thing. Mama couldn't stop smiling.

And even if I don't want to admit it, I'm excited too. Once we're on the steamboat, it'll only be a few more days before we're in Kansas!

Hattie

It was late afternoon by the time the Exodusters climbed the last hill. Below them flowed the Mississippi River, big and mighty. A large wharf stuck out into the water, its dark wood planks wet and shining.

And stretching up and down the bank was an enormous tent city. Hundreds of black people sat in groups and cooked over campfires, their ragged tents flapping in the evening breeze. The air smelled of wood smoke, burnt food, and human waste.

Slowly, Hattie and the Exodusters picked their way down the hill into the camp. The group passed an elderly man seated next to a tent, eating something out of a tin can.

"Is this where we catch the steamboat to Kansas?" Ferguson asked. The man wiped his mouth on his sleeve and tossed the can into some weeds.

"There ain't no steamboats to Kansas, nor anywhere else."

Hattie's chest tightened. She gripped Mama's hand.

"What do you mean, no steamboats?" Mama asked, panic in her voice. "The government is supposed to give us free passage to Kansas."

The man gave Mama a pitying look. "All lies," he said, rising painfully. "You might as well go back to where you came from," he continued. "No steamboats have stopped here for nigh on two weeks. And they're not going to."

Chapter Twelve

"We'll get to the bottom of this, don't worry," Mr. Ferguson smiled, trying to be comforting. The group found a patch of land big enough for them all and set up camp. While the women fixed supper, the men went off to find out what was going on.

Hattie stood by their tiny campfire, her eyes burning from the smoke, keeping watch on Abraham and Eliza, the Ferguson baby, and trying not to worry. Surely Singleton hadn't lied to all of them? But then why were there so many people here, waiting?

It was dark by the time Papa and the others got back. The women silently fed everyone tin plates of crispy johnnycakes, made with cornmeal and bacon fat. No one talked until the plates were clean.

"So?" Hattie couldn't stand it any longer. "Was that man telling the truth?" she cried, trying to keep the anger out of her voice. "There's no steamboats?"

"Not exactly," Ferguson replied sullenly, shaking his head. "There are steamboats. But there ain't no free ones. In that, I was dead wrong. The papers were wrong. There's no free passage to Kansas."

"Not only that," Papa continued, pulling Abraham onto his lap. "The steamboats that do pass haven't been stopping, even for those who can pay."

"Then it's over," Mama sat heavily and buried her head in her hands. "I'm so sorry I pushed us into this terrible trip. It's been nothin' but hardship and pain since we left Nashville."

"Mary, it weren't your fault," Papa said softly, putting his hand over Mama's. "We both made this choice."

Abraham pulled at Papa's sleeve and they played peek-a-boo until the little boy laughed with delight. Hattie wished she could be little again, just for a minute. Then she wouldn't be worried or afraid. She wouldn't be homesick, longing for her old life.

"Word is that the government just passed a law that says the steamboats have to take us," Papa continued. "I think it's true. That's why there's so many folks still here."

"How long 'til they get here?" Hattie didn't want to spend one night in this crowded, smelly camp, let alone a week. Or more.

Papa shrugged. "Hard to say. The next steamboat is expected to come tomorrow. We'll see then."

The next morning, the whole camp was buzzing with the news that a steamboat was on its way. By early afternoon, people began gathering along the landing. Hattie had just put the kettle on the fire when a voice rang out, clear across the camp.

"Steamboat a'comin'!"

A ragged cheer went up from the crowd. Far downriver, Hattie glimpsed a smudge of smoke in the sky. Soon, a tiny white dot appeared beneath it.

It grew larger as it slowly paddled its way upriver, shining so bright in the sun that Hattie had to shade her eyes to look at it. Its colorful flags snapped in the breeze as black smoke billowed into the blue sky.

"I'm going down to the wharf to see what's going on," Papa said casually. He, Mr. Cooper, and Mr. Ferguson headed down the hill as the steamboat approached. Hattie could see hundreds of black people crammed on every deck. There were so many people on board that it seemed the boat might sink into the muddy water. When the boat reached the dock, the huge paddles slowed to a stop.

A white man in a crisp blue uniform stepped off the boat onto the landing and addressed the hopeful crowd. Their camp was too far up the hill for Hattie to hear what he said, but after a few minutes, the crowd began to mutter and shuffle, the happy mood broken. A few people pushed through the crowd and boarded the boat. The rest simply stood there as the huge steamboat paddles roared back to life. With a belch of smoke, the steamboat churned through the brown water and on upriver. The crowd slowly broke up, leaving nothing but muddy footprints.

Papa returned to camp, grim-faced.

"What is it?" Mama had her hand over her heart, as if it couldn't bear any more bad news. Hattie held her breath.

"The good news is that the new law is working," Papa said. "All those folks were Exodusters like us. The bad news is that the boat was full."

"And," he continued, "The steamboat captains are chargin' twice what a ticket should cost."

"How much?" Hattie asked, half afraid to find out.

"Five dollars. Each."

Hattie and Mama gasped.

"What are we gonna do, Nat?" Mama asked. "We don't have that kind of money."

Without thinking, Hattie felt the hem of her dress. The five-dollar bill crinkled softly under her fingers. Should she tell her parents about the money? It was nowhere near enough for all of them. *No*, she thought. *Not yet*.

For the rest of the evening, everyone talked. Papa wanted to stick around for a few more days. Maybe the captains would come to their senses, he thought. Mr. Ferguson thought maybe the government would find out about this mistreatment and do something about it. Mama wasn't so sure.

"Maybe it's time to admit this was a mistake," she said sadly as she scrubbed the supper dishes. "We could settle around here somewhere, I suppose."

"But we're still in Tennessee," Papa replied. "It ain't going to be no better for us here than it was in Nashville."

Much later, after everyone else had gone to bed, Papa pulled Mama and Hattie aside. "I have another idea," he said. "I'm going to Memphis to find work."

Hattie's heart almost stopped.

"But you swore you'd never work for another person again in your life!" she cried.

Papa looked stricken. "Yes, I did," he said slowly. "But remember what that Mavis woman told you?"

Hattie nodded, too angry and miserable to say it out loud.

"Well, then." Papa laid out his plan. He would find work as a blacksmith in Memphis until he'd earned enough for the tickets. Mama, Hattie, and Abraham would stay behind in camp.

"I expect I'll be gone a few weeks, maybe a month at most."

"A month!" Hattie yelped. "We cain't live in this filthy camp a month!"

"I'm sorry," Papa said, reaching for her hand.

Hattie jerked away.

"This is all your fault!" she cried. "Why did you make Rees mad? Why? If it weren't for that, we'd still be home and I'd be in school! You ruined everything!"

May 18, 1879

Dear Diary,

I'm ashamed of myself. When Papa told us he was going to leave us in camp, something just broke inside me. All the anger I'd been carrying around since we left burst out like fire. I ran through the camp to the river. It's a wonder I didn't fall in someone's campfire along the way. When I got there I sank to my knees in the mud, I didn't care. I cried so hard I couldn't breathe.

It was almost dark by the time the tears stopped. I felt empty and dried out, like an old cornhusk.

Someone sat down next to me and I didn't have to look to know it was Papa. We were quiet for a time.

"I'm sorry," we both said at once.

I told him I didn't mean what I said about Rees.

He told me I was right to be upset. That if he'd just gone along and allowed Rees to cheat him, we wouldn'ta left.

"But the price was too high," he said. "Do you understand?"

He said that if he let Rees get away with it, other folks with hearts as dark as his would try to cheat him too. He said he needed to have respect for himself. If he'd let Rees get away with it, he wouldn'ta been able to look at himself in the mirror.

I understand what he means, I think.

He told me we're never safe in the South. And that he doesn't know what's waiting for us in Kansas, but he knows it'll be better than the life we'll have here.

Mama was rocking Abraham in her lap by the fire when we got back. Papa tucked me into the wagon and kissed my forehead. He told me he won't be gone long, and that we'll be on that steamboat to Kansas before we know it.

I can't sleep. My tears are gone, but there's a lump in my throat that won't go away.

Hattie

Chapter Thirteen

Dear Josephine,

So much has happened since we got to the Mississippi that I almost don't know where to start. When we got here we found a big, dirty camp full of Exodusters waiting to get to Kansas. We also found out that the steamboat captains were charging twice what tickets were worth. So Papa decided to find work in Memphis to pay for them. He's been in Memphis now for almost a month. He found a job at a blacksmith's shop. He says they treat him well and the pay is decent. His boss lets him sleep in the shed. He charges him five cents a night for the blanket.

Yesterday, we took the long walk to Memphis to visit Papa. Memphis is a loud, dirty city. The shop Papa works in is big! The forge fires blaze so hot you can feel the heat halfway to the street. Papa thinks he will have enough money for our steamboat tickets in another week or two. But we have to buy food, so I'm afraid it will take a lot longer to raise the money.

The camp is horrid. When it rains, the ground turns to thick, smelly mud. Clouds of mosquitoes devil us all day and night. One of the women in camp brung us some leaves and told us to rub them on our skin. She said the skeeters wouldn't bother us. It worked!

Sometimes days go by without a steamboat. Then one comes but it's too full to stop. Or it stops, but only takes a few folks.

Folks are running out of money and food. Every day I wake up and more people are gone. Almost all the Exodusters who started with us have left. Only the Coopers and Mr. Ferguson and his wife are still here.

There's a sickness going around the camp. Abraham has it, but me and Mama have been spared so far.

Mama's been helping folks out best she can. She spends hours makin' medicine for folks in camp. She works from dawn 'til long past dark but I don't ever hear one complaint.

I hope Kansas is worth all this trouble and hardship.

Your devoted friend,
Hattie

Hattie folded the paper and put it into her letterbox for safekeeping. Abraham, who was lying next to her, whined and fussed softly. Hattie grabbed a handful of leaves and started rubbing her brother's arms.

"Mama, he's burnin' up!"

"I know, baby," she said, smoothing Abraham's sweaty forehead. "Fevers run hot and quick in young'uns. How are you feelin'?"

Mama pressed the back of her hand to Hattie's forehead. "Cool as a cucumber," she said, relieved. "Go to the river and fetch some water. I'll make up another batch of broth."

Carrying water was the worst chore, but Hattie knew better than to complain. Sighing, she filled the kettle and lugged it back to camp. It was hard not to let the heavy thing bump her legs and splash water on her dress.

Mama gave her a tired smile as she fried slices of silvery white onions in a dab of bacon grease. Hattie was thoroughly sick of the smell of onions, but it was the only medicine anyone had. It was pure luck that Mama had found that bag of onions at one of the abandoned camps. Most of them had been moldy, but she cut away the spots and made them as good as new.

Once the onions were brown and soft, Mama scraped them into a huge pot of simmering water. While it cooked, she set out a bunch of tin cans. She'd found them during another one of her "explorations" around the camp. Mama had scrubbed them clean, sure she'd find a use for them somehow. She didn't waste anything.

When the broth was done, she filled each can.

"You stay here with Abraham. If he fusses, give him some broth."

Hattie watched Mama pick her way from camp to camp, handing out tin cans to anyone who needed it. *She shoulda been a doctor*, Hattie thought suddenly, *instead of a washerwoman*.

It was dark when Mama came back. Abraham had woken up, still hot with fever. He spit out the onion broth and cried so loud that Hattie thought her ears would burst.

"Let me sit with him a spell," Mama said tiredly, pressing a wet cloth around his neck. That seemed to calm him some. Hattie closed her eyes and was instantly asleep.

When Hattie awoke the next morning, the world looked bright and wavy. Every bone in her body seemed to ache. She found Mama at the fire, making more broth.

"I don't feel so good," she said. "I'm hot and cold at once."

Mama felt her forehead. "Lordy, you're sick too." She laid Hattie back down in the tent next to Abraham. She put a cool cloth on Hattie's neck.

Everything looked and sounded strange to Hattie. For a long time, she didn't go to sleep, but she wasn't fully awake either. She tossed and turned, throwing off the blanket, and then wrapping it around her. There were voices outside the tent, but she couldn't understand what they were saying. The world got dark, and then it was so bright, the light hurt her eyes. Someone put a tin cup to her lips, and she gulped cold water. Mama made her sip onion broth out of a tin can.

Abraham felt like a ball of fire beside her. He kicked and cried and made her cry too. Big, rough hands put cold cloths on her head. A familiar voice told her over and over that she'd be just fine.

When she finally woke up, it was nighttime. Abraham was no longer next to her and she was alone, covered in sweat.

"Mama!"

The tent flap flew open and it was Papa, not Mama, who took Hattie into his arms. "Oh, praise be, your fever's broken," he said, hugging her to his chest. "We've been so worried these past three days."

"What are you doing here? Where's Bram?" Hattie's questions poured out of her as Papa gave her a tin cup of water.

"Whoa, slow down. I came as soon as I heard you and Bram was sick," he replied. "Bram is much improved and with your mama."

Hattie gulped down the water and handed the cup back to Papa. "So you'll be going back to Memphis now that we're well," she said dejectedly.

"Not exactly," Papa said. "I got enough money for our passage. I sold Old Jeb and the wagon to a farmer nearby."

Then he said the words Hattie had begun to think she'd never hear again.

"We'll board a steamboat as soon as you're well enough to travel. We're going to Kansas."

Chapter Fourteen

May 31, 1879

Dear Diary,

I think we're finally leaving for Kansas tomorrow! Word is a boat is on its way, and Mama wants to make sure we get on it. It took days for me to feel up to leaving the tent. More than half of the camp had come down with the fever, and Mama's onion soup ran out quick, but she did what she could to nurse the sick.

Mama wants us to get up at sunrise so we can be the first in line. Which means I need to get some rest now.

Hattie

*H*attie stood on the landing, clutching her bundle as the huge steamboat chugged slowly upriver, smoke pouring from its tall smokestack.

The steamboat let out a piercing whistle, and then began to slow. Several rough-looking riverboat crewmen appeared at the railing. They pushed a gangplank from the boat to the landing and tied it with thick ropes. The

captain appeared, the brass buttons on his uniform shining in the morning sun.

He looked out over our hopeful faces, his wiry white eyebrows furrowed.

Papa stepped forward. "We have four," he said. "Me, my wife, and my two young'uns." The captain squinted his eyes and looked them over.

"Fare is five dollars each," he said finally. "Full price for everyone."

Papa nodded and handed over the money.

The captain quickly counted it then nodded, waving them forward. Mama smiled and squeezed Hattie's hand as they stepped onto the gangplank. They were halfway up when the captain stepped in front of Papa.

"You can't bring that aboard," he said, pointing to the tool chest.

"These are the tools of my trade," Papa said, trying to keep his voice steady. "I'm a blacksmith. I've brung them all the way from Nashville. I'd be obliged if you'd allow me to take them."

"Too much weight," the captain said. "If it isn't necessities like food and clothing, you can't bring it aboard. Maybe the next boat will let you have them."

Hattie clutched Mama's hand, her heart beating wildly.

"And when will that boat be here?"

"I have no idea," the captain replied irritably. "Either leave them behind or step away."

"Come on the boat, Nat," Mama said, holding out her hand. "We'll make do. We always have."

The Fergusons were behind Papa, waiting to board. Mr. Ferguson stepped forward. He glanced at Papa, and then turned to the captain.

"Would a dollar be enough to get that box on board?" he asked in a low voice. The captain glanced at Papa, then away.

"Two."

"John, I won't allow it," Papa said sternly. "You won't be able to pay your own passage."

"You kept food in our bellies on the road, "Mr. Ferguson said. "Mary nursed my Beulah and the baby back from sickness. I owe you plenty more than this. We'll find a way." He handed the captain the money, which disappeared into his pocket.

Papa and Mr. Ferguson shook hands as Mama and Mrs. Ferguson hugged tightly, tears on their cheeks. The Fergusons stepped aside as Hattie and her family made their way up the gangplank.

More families were allowed on board. The Coopers pushed through the crowds to the other side of the boat. Then the captain held up his hand. "That's all," he announced. A gasp went through the crowd.

"There's plenty of room on the decks!" one man shouted.

"We've been a' waitin' for weeks!" another cried.

"You'll just have to wait longer." The captain disappeared as the crew untied the ropes. The boat shuddered as the engine came to life. Hattie gripped the railing and watched the Fergusons pick their way back into camp. At the last minute, Mrs. Ferguson turned and waved. Hattie waved back madly.

"Do you think we'll ever see them again?" Hattie asked as the boat picked up speed.

"The good Lord willin'," Mama replied. They watched until the camp was a tiny speck in the distance. Then Mama sighed.

"Let's get settled and see what's what on this boat."

Dear Josephine,

I can't believe we're finally on our way again. It took darn near a whole week to get well. I still feel wobbly and lightheaded from time to time. I'm not sure if it's from the sickness or the excitement of being on a real steamboat.

So far the weather has been fine, which is lucky for us. All the passengers have to sleep outside on the deck. We stopped twice and picked up more Exodusters. I heard one crewman say there were more than three hundred of us on board! The captain says we should make St. Louis by the end of the week if the weather holds.

Your devoted friend,
Hattie

The decks were choked with Exodusters. They stood, sat, and laid down shoulder to shoulder, taking up every inch of the deck. Hattie desperately sought a little spot to herself, away from the hundreds of strangers.

She found it one day as she was exploring. Behind a small door, Hattie discovered the hold, where all the crew's supplies were stored. She crawled between the huge crates and barrels until she came to a roomy spot where no one could see her. She snuck away to the hold every day to read or write.

Most of the time, she was alone. Once in a while, a crewman would appear. He would rummage around for whatever he was looking for, then leave. It was fun to be in her special hiding place when that happened. So when she heard two people in the hold one afternoon, she held her breath and listened.

"Two more days and we'll be in Saint Louie," one of them said. "I can't wait."

"Me neither," the other replied, opening a crate with a bang. "The captain better give us our full pay this time or they'll be a mutiny."

"Oh, he will. He's got a scheme that'll make us all some extra money."

The crewman explained that the captain planned to put every Exoduster off the boat the next morning, miles from St. Louis! Only those who could pay would be allowed to stay on board.

The other man chuckled.

"That old fox! I knowed he wasn't happy about that new law that said we had to pick up all them black folks. So he gets this riffraff off our boat and he lines his pockets with extra money!"

Hattie's ears were ringing as the men left. *How could we walk all the way to St. Louis?* Mama's belly had gotten a lot bigger in the last few weeks with the new baby. She was in no condition to walk that far. They left their tent and all their camping supplies behind. All they had were their clothes. The unfairness of it all made her so angry she wanted to scream.

She crept out of her hiding place and headed back to her family on deck. *Should I tell them what I heard? What if it weren't true? Then I'd worry them for no reason. Besides, maybe we do have enough money left to stay on the boat.* That thought comforted Hattie a little. She decided to keep this bit of news to herself, for now.

That evening after supper, Mama began digging through their bags. Papa came back from a walk around the deck with Abraham.

"Nat," she said in a low voice. "Did you take my red handkerchief? The one I'd tied our money in?"

"Not that I'm aware," Papa replied, echoing her worry. "Why?"

"It ain't here," she said, panic creeping in. "I've torn this bag apart and I cain't find it."

They quietly searched all their bags, but no red handkerchief turned up. Mama's shoulders slumped.

"That was the last of the money we got from selling Old Jeb and the wagon," she said dejectedly. "We've been robbed, that's a fact."

"I got a little set by, enough for food when we get to St. Louis," Papa said reassuringly. "We're to meet Singleton, remember? He'll take care of us."

"But we was supposed to be in St. Louis weeks ago. What if he ain't there?"

"We'll make do," Papa said, putting his hand on Mama's shoulder.

I can't bear to tell them about the captain's plan now, Hattie thought, *but how can I keep it to myself?* Her mind was jumbled. Then one thought burst out of the confusion. Of course.

It was the only way.

Chapter Fifteen

*H*er parents were too busy talking to notice her slip quietly away. She went back to the hold. When she was safely inside, she tugged at the ragged hem of her dress until the stitches gave way. The damp, worn five-dollar bill dropped into her hand.

She didn't know if it would be enough, but she had to try. She'd never bribed someone before. *What if it didn't work? Worse, what if he got angry?*

Hattie pushed those thoughts away and took a deep breath. The captain always smoked a cigar on the upper deck in the evening. She climbed the stairs and looked around. Sure enough, there he was. He leaned on the railing, scowling, a brown cigar clamped between his teeth. Below him, hundreds of Exodusters crushed cheek-to-jowl on every deck.

Hattie paused. When he saw her, he frowned.

"What are you doing up here?" the captain demanded. "Get on back down where you belong."

"Mr. Captain, sir," Hattie began in her most polite voice. Inside, her heart was hammering madly. "I wanted to thank you for takin' us to St. Louis. It means a lot to my family."

The captain peered at her and didn't say a word. Smoke curled from the cigar and disappeared into the evening air.

"To show our appreciation, I wanted to give you something. Just so's we know we'll be landing in St. Louis day after tomorrow."

She opened her book of poetry and pulled out the five-dollar bill. The captain's bushy eyebrows popped up in surprise.

"What's this?" he said gruffly. "Who put you up to this?"

"No one, sir. We're all just thankful for your kindness. It's so important that we get to St. Louis, my mama being in her state and all."

The captain didn't answer. Hattie hoped he'd say something kind.

He looked closely at her. "Is that your book?"

Hattie nodded, surprised. "Why, yes sir," she replied, the words tumbling out. It was like she had no control over her tongue as she told him about Miss Banneker and how she hoped to be a teacher one day.

Her voice trailed off. There wasn't anything more to say. The captain stared out at the water, chewing on the end of the cigar until it was a soggy mess. Then he sighed and slowly opened his palm. Hattie's heart sank as she pressed the money in his hand. He slid it into his pocket and nodded.

"Thank you," Hattie whispered. At the bottom of the steps, she stopped and looked back. The captain was gone.

Did it work? He took the money, so Hattie thought it did. She should have been pleased. But instead, she felt sad and uncomfortable, like she'd done something mean and gotten away with it. Mavis Robinson's voice drifted through her mind.

It ain't no sin to do what you have to do to care for the ones you love.

Maybe not, Hattie thought as she made her way back to her family. *But why did it have to feel so bad?*

When she returned, Mama and Abraham were asleep. Papa rested against a coil of rope, snoring softly. She looked at their tired, dirty faces and loved them so much, it felt as though her heart would break. Mavis was right. She'd do anything for them.

I'll tell them when we get to St. Louis, she promised herself as she settled in. When we're safe. She closed her eyes, but sleep would not come. So she watched the stars as the steamboat carried them closer to St. Louis.

June 4, 1879

Dear Diary,

I didn't get much sleep last night. The butterflies in my stomach woke me up at dawn. Everything seemed normal. Mama fixed breakfast. I watched the crew but they went about their business like they always do. I almost told Mama what I'd

done a hundred times. But something stopped me.
Guilt, maybe. Or just plain old fear.

I tried to take my mind off things by
reading my book, but that didn't help.
Word spread that we'd be in St. Louis by
tomorrow morning. It's almost suppertime
and my nerves are so on edge I can't sit still.
Is the captain going to do it? I can hardly
stand to look at all the hopeful faces.

Hattie

❖ ❖ ❖

"What's got into you?" Mama asked as they ate.
"You've been jumpy as a frog all day!"

Hattie shrugged and said nothing. The boat sailed
on. She longed to tell her parents what was going on. But
she couldn't bring herself to add to their worries. She was
afraid too. Afraid they'd be angry at her for what she'd
done.

After supper, a figure pushed through the mass of people standing, sitting, and lying on the deck. He looked here and there, as if he were searching for someone. When his eyes lit on Hattie, he came straight to her.

It was one of the crewmen.

"Are you the girl who reads?" he asked.

She was so shocked, she couldn't make a sound. She nodded.

"Here," he said, shoving a book in her hands. He turned and disappeared into the crowd.

"What was that all about?" Papa asked.

"I—I don't know," Hattie stammered. She turned the book over in her hands. It had been well loved. The leather had cracked in several places. The pages were dog-eared and worn.

Leaves of Grass, she read on the spine. A book of poetry. Something had been slid between the well-loved pages. It was a small photograph of a white girl. She sat primly on a chair, a book cradled in one arm and a doll in the other. Hattie could just make out the words on the cover: *Leaves of Grass*.

A few words were written in spidery handwriting on the back of the photo.

This is Victoria, my book reader. She died when she was nine. Thank you for reminding me of her. Godspeed to you and your family.

When Hattie lifted the photo out of the book, a piece of paper fluttered to the deck. It was her five-dollar bill.

"What in tarnation is going on, Hypatia Florence Jacobs?"

With a sob, the whole story spilled out, as if a dam had broken. The worry and fear that weighed her down seemed to wash away with every word. When she finished, Papa looked thunderstruck.

"I'd heard a whisper of something like that," he said slowly. "But it seems you changed his mind."

"My brave girl," Mama crooned, holding Hattie tight. "Don't you ever think you cain't tell us something like this." Hattie nodded. She leaned against Mama and closed her eyes, and said a prayer for the little girl who loved poetry, and the steamboat captain who had loved her.

Chapter Sixteen

The steamboat was scheduled to arrive a little before noon, but Hattie had been at the railing since dawn. By the time the city came into view, every Exoduster on the boat was ready. Excitement was thick in the air.

With a long, piercing whistle and a belch of smoke, the steamboat paddled to a stop at the wharf. Crewmen lowered the gangplank and people jostled to get off.

A well-dressed black man appeared out of the crowd. "Are you one of the Exodusters?" he asked kindly. "I'm Adam, I'm with the Colored Men's Land Association of St. Louis. Our organization is providing food, clothing, and a place to stay for the new arrivals."

They followed Adam a few blocks to a large church. Dozens of people milled about the hallways. Hattie recognized many of their fellow steamboat passengers talking and laughing, relief and hope in their faces. Adam showed them to a small room with cots and a washbasin.

"There's a kitchen out back," he explained. "Food's waiting. Welcome to St. Louis!"

When he left, Mama sank gratefully onto one of the cots, her arms around her expanding belly. "Lordy, it's good to be off a moving boat!" she sighed.

After they'd washed up, they went in search of the kitchen. They got their bowls of stew and fresh bread and found seats at the long tables set up outside.

"Jacobs! Nat Jacobs!" Singleton strode up to their table. "Adam said you were here. I'm so relieved to see you. When I heard about the trouble with the steamboats, I feared you'd give up and go back to Nashville."

Hattie slowly ate her stew and listened to Papa tell the story of their adventures.

"I'm not surprised, Jacobs," Singleton commented, frowning. "Your story sounds like many others. I'm glad you made it."

"I'm not sure what we're going to do now," Papa said. "I reckon we need to decide where to settle."

"Have you thought about the town of Nicodemus?" Singleton asked. "That would be a good town for your family. It's a young town, founded in 1877. They need a blacksmith, that's for sure. Plenty of land for farming. They've got a school."

Hattie's ears perked up at the word *school*.

"Did you hear that, Nat?" Mama asked. "A town of black folks. We can have the farm you always wanted."

"Are you sure about this, Singleton?" Papa was skeptical.

"If you don't believe me, read this." Singleton handed Mama a newspaper clipping from the Lawrence, Kansas, newspaper.

A correspondent of the Chicago Tribune has just visited the colony of Nicodemus and gives us the following items concerning it:

It is the capital or head center of a black colony in Graham County. The settlement consists of about 125 families comprising a population of about 700 souls scattered over an area of twelve miles. Nicodemus has a post office, store, hotel, land office, etc.

"A post office, store, and a hotel!" Mama looked up at Papa excitedly.

"Well then," Papa said, smiling, "Nicodemus it is."

Hattie jumped up and threw her arms around Papa. "I wonder what the school will look like! Are there many children in town?" The questions tumbled out so fast that both Papa and Singleton chuckled.

"We'll need to arrange your trip to Kansas and make sure you have provisions," Singleton said.

Over the next few days, Hattie and her family rested and prepared for the final leg of their long journey. One morning, several women appeared at the church with donated clothing and supplies. Singleton came by one afternoon and handed Papa four train tickets.

"You'll take the train to Topeka," he said. "When you get there, one of my agents will help you purchase a wagon, horses, and other supplies. From there, you'll go to Nicodemus."

Hattie had never been on a train before, and the thought made her giddy with excitement.

A week later, everything was ready and it was time to go. Singleton drove them to the train station, which was just as crowded as the wharf had been.

"Thank you," Papa said to Singleton, shaking his hand warmly.

"A better life is waiting there for you," Singleton replied, winking at Hattie. "I guarantee it."

They boarded the train and found their places. Hattie couldn't contain her excitement; she bounced on the seat until Mama had to tell her to stop. She leaned out the window as the train pulled away from the station. Steam and smoke poured from the engine. She watched St. Louis fade into the distance, and it was like all their troubles and hardships faded away with it. She sat back and smiled, clutching her two precious books in her arms.

Chapter Seventeen

Dear Josephine,

I'm writing to you from a real Kansas prairie! It's like an ocean of green. It stretches all the way to the horizon. At night there are so many stars that I can almost read by their light.

We left Topeka a week ago. The train ride from St. Louis to Topeka was long and boring. But I was grateful for the train. I am tired of riding in wagons! When we arrived, a nice lady met us at the station just like Mr. Singleton promised. She helped us find lodging and gave Papa enough money to buy a wagon and a team of horses. We needed the team to pull the plow on our new farm!

While we were in Topeka, we met other families who are going to Nicodemus. One of them was

Mr. Ferguson and his family from Tennessee! We were right pleased to see them. I wasn't happy to find out it was another long wagon trip from Topeka to Nicodemus. Once we get to Nicodemus, I swear I'm never going to ride in a wagon again!

We've been on the prairie now for five days. Last night we had a bit of a fright. After supper a group of riders appeared. At first we thought they were up to no good. But they were soldiers. Not only that, but they were black soldiers! Papa said they're called buffalo soldiers. Mama fixed them supper and they were grateful for the food. One of them fashioned a toy horse for Abraham from a stick of wood. He was happy, but I was happier that he wasn't cryin' no more.

Only a few more days in this wagon and we'll be in Nicodemus. I'm so excited I can't stand it.

Your devoted friend,
Hattie

$\mathcal{F}$inally, the last day on the road dawned. Today, Hattie and her family would arrive in Nicodemus. Mile after mile, they got closer. Excitement ran so high that Hattie couldn't stand to ride in the wagon for another minute. She skipped beside the wagon and kept a lookout for the town.

In late morning, one of the men who'd ridden ahead came galloping back. "Just another mile or two!" he whooped. Everyone cheered.

"Papa, can I please run ahead?" Hattie begged. Papa smiled and nodded. Hattie took off across the prairie, her head barely visible above the waves of green grass. She ran up and down gentle, rolling hills to the highest one, and stopped, breathing hard.

Nicodemus.

She stood there until the rest of the group had caught up. Mama jumped from the wagon and ran as best she could to her, laughing with happiness. She looked out and stopped dead. The laughter died in the air. Her smile disappeared, replaced by the same look of shock that Hattie felt.

There were no trim houses or buildings. No farms. Nicodemus sat in the middle of a brown patch of prairie that looked as if someone had scraped the grass clean away. A few sad-looking clapboard structures huddled together, the only sign that anyone was here at all.

The happy mood died. Slowly, the group made their way into town.

"What is all that smoke coming up from the ground?" Hattie asked.

Mama shook her head, her eyes filled with tears. "I don't know, baby."

"Them's houses," Mr. Ferguson said softly. "Dugouts."

Mama looked at him like he'd grown another head. "Do you mean to tell me that the people live in the dirt? Under the ground?"

Mr. Ferguson didn't reply. He gave Papa the saddest, sorriest look Hattie ever saw.

Mama collapsed into Papa's arms, sobbing uncontrollably.

"Oh dear Lord, what have we done?" she screamed. Hattie began to sob too.

Papa tried to put his arms around Mama, but she pushed him away. She sank into the grass, her sobs coming in great gasps.

They all stood silently watching Mama, their own tears of grief and disappointment flowing. After a few moments, Papa gently took Mama by the arm and hauled her to her feet.

"Now you see here, Mary," he began, stern but not unkind. He scooped a handful of dirt and put it in front of her face. "Do you know what this is?"

Mama gave him a puzzled look, her face streaked with dirt and tears.

"It is free ground. You are standing on free ground. Free! For the first time in our lives, we're truly free. This ain't a time to be sad. We brung our young'uns here to be free. We didn't have that when we was their age, but we can give them that here."

Mama stared at him. Then slowly, she nodded. He threw the dirt down and slowly raised her up.

"Let's go find the mayor of this town," Papa said.

Mama sniffed and wiped her face with the hem of her dress. As they went into town, black people seemed to appear out of nowhere. They surrounded the Exodusters.

"Welcome to Nicodemus, friend."

"We're so glad you made it."

"We're here to help you, don't you worry."

A woman with a wide smile took Mama's arm. "I'm Jenny Fletcher. My husband, Zachary, is the secretary of the Nicodemus Town Company." She saw the despair on Mama's face and smiled sympathetically.

"I know it's a shock at first," she said as she led them away. "But believe you me, this is one good town! You'll be glad you came."

She took them to a house, which was little more than a big hole dug out of the side of a small hill. The roof was made of blocks of sod, with the chimney pipe sticking up out of the dirt. When they stepped inside, Hattie got a shock. It looked like any other well-kept cabin, with rugs on the dirt floor and a pretty lace cloth on the table. A wooden bed stood in one corner, made up with clean sheets and a homemade quilt. A small iron stove sat on the other side.

"This here will be yours," Mrs. Fletcher said. "It ain't much, but it's dry and it stays cool on hot prairie days."

She bustled around, helping Papa bring in their bags from the wagon, and chattering the whole time. "We've all got lumber coming to build proper houses, you can order some when you're ready. You're the new blacksmith, right?"

Papa looked a little confused, but nodded. Mrs. Fletcher beamed.

"So glad to hear it! Zachary is about to start building the new livery stable, and you'll be sorely needed when it's done."

"Where's the hotel? And the school?" Hattie asked hesitantly. "The newspaper said you had those here."

"And we do! The hotel is that building on Main Street. The school is in my house! Every day, eight o'clock sharp." Hattie tried to keep the disappointment off her face, but it didn't work. Mrs. Fletcher smiled kindly.

"A schoolhouse is on our list to build too," she said. "Nicodemus ain't been here long." Mrs. Fletcher smiled. "Come to my place for supper. We'll talk more then. Again, welcome to Nicodemus!" She turned with a flourish and was gone.

The dugout was dark and smelled of earth and grass. Papa lit the kerosene lamp on the table. Mama was silent, looking around the room.

In the quiet, Hattie heard the most unexpected sound. Laughter.

It started with a chuckle, and then it grew until Mama's laughter filled the dugout. Hattie couldn't help but smile, her own laughter bubbling up like a fountain. Papa chuckled too. Abraham didn't understand what was going on, so he jumped up and down, waving his wooden horse.

It took a while, but finally, they laughed themselves out. Mama put her arms around Papa's neck.

"It ain't what I expected," she said, "but we all made it here, and we're alive."

Papa wrapped Hattie and Abraham in one arm. He put his other hand gently on Mama's belly.

"And we're free. That's as good a start as any, don't you think?"

Chapter Eighteen

ONE YEAR LATER

"Mama, I'm home!"

Hattie tossed her books on the kitchen table as Mama stirred a pot on the stove. Delicious smells wafted across the dugout.

"Where's Papa?" she asked, bending down to pick up baby Isabel, who was lying in her cradle. "Dang, you're getting heavy!" Isabel waved her chubby baby arms and gave Hattie a drool-y grin.

"He'll be home from the stable soon," Mama replied, wiping her hands on her apron. "There's a letter for you on the table."

Hattie instantly recognized Josephine's loopy handwriting. She ripped open the envelope and read quickly.

"They're almost here!" Hattie cried, looking at the postmark. "She sent this from Kansas City. Oh, Mama, I cain't wait to see her!"

Mama smiled. "It'll be good to see them again," she replied. "Now go wash up for supper."

Papa and Abraham arrived from the stable, and they all cleaned up at the water pump out back. Abraham chattered about the horses and a litter of kittens that lived under the stable. Hattie told them about her perfect score on her history exam.

There was an envelope beside Papa's place when he sat down. It was from the bank.

Hattie couldn't stand the suspense. "What's it say?"

"Well, it looks like the bank's approved us to buy a land grant."

Mama almost knocked over the stewpot with surprise. "So we're really getting the farm? I cain't believe it!"

Hattie and Abraham squealed and danced around the room until Isabel started crying from the commotion. Papa scooped her up, grinning.

"We'll go to the land office tomorrow. I can hardly believe this day has finally come."

The next afternoon, the whole family, dressed in their Sunday best, walked to town. They stopped to greet friends and neighbors along the way. Most of them were Exodusters just like them. Some had been there since Nicodemus was founded. Others had arrived only a few weeks ago. Everyone fussed over Isabel and admired the tortoise shell comb in Mama's hair.

Hattie marveled at how much the town had changed in just one year. The two-story general store stood majestically over Main Street. Several other buildings and a church clustered nearby. Trim white cottages sat on the outskirts of town. Farther out, modest farmsteads dotted the prairie. Beyond that, miles of land. Some of that would soon be theirs!

Inside the land office, Papa's hand trembled as he filled out the claim forms. Hattie burst with pride as she watched her father's lifelong dream come true. But when it came time to put his signature on the forms, he folded the pages and put them in his pocket.

"What are you doing, Nat?" Mama asked.

"You'll see," was all he'd say.

Puzzled, they followed him home. Mama had made a cake to celebrate, but the room was quiet as everyone ate.

"I've been thinking," Papa began. His voice got low and strange in a way Hattie had never heard. "I've been thinking about my name. Our name. Jacobs."

He turned to Hattie. "Did you know that slaves used to take the last name of their owners?" She shook her head.

"Jacobs was the name of the white man who owned my family when I was born," he continued. "After the war, I didn't really think about it much. Nor did it seem bothersome when I married your mama."

Papa gazed at Mama, who looked at him with love shining in her eyes. "But since we've been in Kansas, I've pondered it quite a bit. And I've decided that I'm tired of having a slave's name. I want the name of a free man."

"You want to change our name?" Hattie exclaimed, horrified and excited at once. "What would we change it to?"

"I don't know. That's why I'm talking to you now."

They spent a lively hour thinking of names for the family. Abraham, who had just learned the alphabet, proudly suggested everything from "Adams" to "Zeb." They wrote down dozens of possibilities, but none seemed right. Hattie was about ready to run to the school and fetch Mrs. Fletcher's dictionary when Mama spoke up.

"My granny used to tell me a story," she said softly, almost hesitantly. "A long time ago, her mama, my great-grandmother, lived in Africa. She was stolen from her family and brought here to be a slave."

Mama got a faraway look in her eyes, remembering. "The only thing Granny knew about her mama was that her African name was Tunnar. So maybe that could be a name for us."

Papa placed his hand over Mama's. "I think that's a fine name."

He looked at Hattie.

She nodded, smiling. "I like it too."

He pulled the papers from his pocket and smoothed them on the table. With a steady hand, he signed his new name, Nathanial Tunnar.

A feeling of happiness swept through Hattie like a fresh wind.

"I feel like giving thanks." She rose and led everyone outside. It had started raining, but no one cared. The family held hands as she spoke.

"Today, this family threw off the last chains of slavery that bound us," she began. She gazed at her family. They had all gone through so much to be here.

"The Jacobs family is gone. This Kansas rain is falling from heaven on a truly free family, the Tunnar family."

"And it feels like sunshine."

Author's Note

This is a work of fiction, but the Great Exodus of 1879 was a real event, and the Exodusters were real people. Hattie and her family represent the thousands of former slaves and their families who left Tennessee, Kentucky, and Louisiana for the promise of free land and better lives.

Although the Great Exodus was an important moment in African American history, there are surprisingly few books and sources about it. The best-known book on the Exoduster movement is *Exodusters: Black Migration to Kansas After Reconstruction* by Nell Irvin Painter. Other sources, such as the National Archives, the Library of Congress, the Kansas Historical Society, and the National Park Service, have collections of documents and items relating to this movement. I've also relied on historical newspapers from the time, eyewitness accounts, and testimony by Benjamin Singleton to the US Congress in 1880, titled "Negro Exodus from the Southern States."

The Great Exodus, also known as the Kansas Exodus or the Colored Exodus, had its beginnings long before the spring of 1879. During the Civil War, tens of thousands of African Americans were enslaved in the South. When the Civil War ended, those slaves were set free, although it took months for word to reach some states. The Thirteenth Amendment, passed in December 1865, abolished slavery for all time.

Many expected their lives to get better after the war. But these newly freed people faced racism and poverty so great, it couldn't be overcome. White men still owned most farmland and rented out parcels to African Americans. They cheated these black tenant farmers. African Americans knew they were being treated unfairly. They began looking for ways to get out of the South.

For some, Kansas seemed to be the answer. Kansas was a free state. In 1862, during the Civil War, Congress passed the Homestead Act. It allowed all US citizens the right to apply to the government for 160 acres of land. After the war was over, Congress passed the Fourteenth Amendment to the Constitution. It gave citizenship to all former slaves. African Americans could now get free land!

Some African American businessmen saw this as an opportunity to create their own communities in Kansas.

Benjamin "Pap" Singleton was one of them. He was born into slavery in Tennessee in 1809. He escaped to the North, but returned to Nashville after the war. His dream was to create settlements where African Americans could homestead the land and live in peace. He traveled through the South, speaking at churches and in meetings. He passed out thousands of fliers encouraging families to move to Kansas. With his help, hundreds of African Americans from Tennessee followed him to Kansas between 1877 and 1879.

In the spring of 1879, the idea to go to Kansas really caught fire in many southern African American communities. Tens of thousands of people packed up everything they owned and set off for Kansas. These emigrants were called Exodusters, after the exodus of Jews from Egypt in the Bible. They landed in St. Louis, Topeka, and other Kansas towns, with few supplies and no real idea of what to do next. There were so many people to take care of that local businessmen created organizations to help them get to settlements farther west in Kansas.

One of the largest, and most famous, of the Kansas settlements was Nicodemus. A group of settlers founded the town in 1877, including Jenny and Zachary Fletcher, and by the year Hattie's family arrived, the town had hundreds of residents. The town grew strong during the 1880s. It had two newspapers, a hotel, and even an ice cream parlor. But the town slowly began to die. It turned out that the land was not well-suited for farming. The railroads refused to build stops in the town. People moved away. By the early twentieth century, Nicodemus was little more than a ghost town. Today, Nicodemus is part of the National Park Service. Its five remaining buildings are historic landmarks.

It's estimated that by 1879, more than fifty thousand Exodusters made their way to Kansas. Many of them successfully built settlements, farms, and better lives. But thousands never made it to their promised land. Instead, they found work in the large towns, or quietly returned to the South. By the mid-1880s, the Great Exodus was over.

Photos

Exodusters waiting to board a steamboat in the late 1870s

Homesteaders in Nicodemus, Kansas, date unknown

Exoduster Movement, 1879

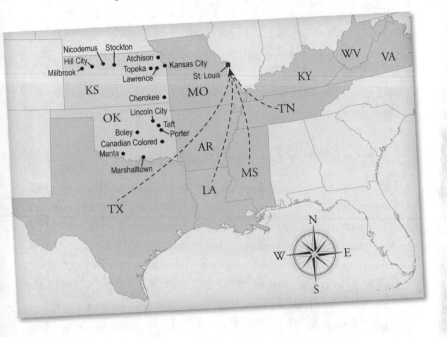

The majority of the Exodusters migrated from Tennessee (mostly prior to 1879), Louisiana, Mississippi, and Texas. Far fewer Exodusters came from Kentucky, Alabama, and Georgia.

Most of the Exodusters arrived in St. Louis first. They then traveled to their destination in Kansas by foot, riverboat, or train. Exodusters settled in Atchison, Kansas City, Topeka, Wyandotte, and Lawrence.

About the Author

Allison Lassieur once lived in Tennessee and traveled the path Hattie and her family might have followed from Nashville to the banks of the Mississippi River near Memphis. Today, she lives in upstate New York and shares a 110-year-old house with her husband, daughter, three dogs, two cats, and more history books than she can count.

About the Consultant

Dr. Sharlene Sinegal-DeCuir is an Associate Professor of History at Xavier University of Louisiana. Throughout her academic career, she has focused on the New South period of American history through the Civil Rights Movement, with particular interest on African American activism in Louisiana. She has been featured on MSNBC with Al Sharpton, WBOK New Orleans Talk Radio, the New Orleans *Times-Picayune*, is a contributor for the PBS show "We'll Meet Again" with Ann Curry, and published a *New York Times* Op-Ed article.

About the Illustrator

Eric Freeberg has illustrated over twenty-five books for children, and has created work for magazines and ad campaigns. He was a winner of the 2010 London Book Fair's Children's Illustration Competition; the 2010 Holbein Prize for Fantasy Art, International Illustration Competition, Japan Illustrators Association; Runner-Up, 2013 SCBWI Magazine Merit Award; Honorable Mention, 2009 SCBWI Don Freeman Portfolio Competition; and 2nd Prize, 2009 Clymer Museum's Annual Illustration Invitational. He was also a winner of the Elizabeth Greenshields Foundation Award.